SEAL'S HELLION (SPECIAL FORCES OPERATION ALPHA)

BLACK EAGLE 3

LYNNE ST. JAMES

This book is a work of fiction. Names, characters, places, and incidents are products of the author's imagination or used fictitiously. Any resemblance to actual events or locales or persons living or dead is entirely coincidental.

© 2019 ACES PRESS, LLC. ALL RIGHTS RESERVED

No part of this work may be used, stored, reproduced or transmitted without written permission from the publisher except for brief quotations for review purposes as permitted by law.
This book is licensed for your personal enjoyment only. This book may not be re-sold or given away to other people. If you would like to share this book with another person, please purchase an additional copy for each recipient. If you're reading this book and did not purchase it, or it was not purchased for your use only, please purchase your own copy.

Copyright © 2019 by Lynne St. James
Cover Art Copyright © 2019 by Lynne St. James
Published by Aces Press
Cover by Lori Jackson Designs
Created in the United States

Dear Readers,

Welcome to the Special Forces: Operation Alpha Fan-Fiction world!

If you are new to this amazing world, in a nutshell the author wrote a story using one or more of my characters in it. Sometimes that character has a major role in the story, and other times they are only mentioned briefly. This is perfectly legal and allowable because they are going through Aces Press to publish the story.

This book is entirely the work of the author who wrote it. While I might have assisted with brainstorming and other ideas about which of my characters to use, I didn't have any part in the process or writing or editing the story.

I'm proud and excited that so many authors loved my characters enough that they wanted to write them into their own story. Thank you for supporting them, and me!

READ ON!

Xoxo

Susan Stoker

NOTE TO READERS

I read Susan's books and love her characters as much as all of you. When I had the opportunity to write in her world I was thrilled. Being able to include her amazing SEAL team in my books has been so much fun.

I hope you enjoy my take on her characters. I try to keep true to Susan's vision, but I take certain allowances for the purpose of my stories.

In ***SEAL's Hellion,*** John "Tex" Keegan, Matthew "Wolf" Steel and his wife, Caroline make guest appearances.

I hope you enjoy ***SEAL's Hellion.*** Remember, the best way to thank an author is to leave a review.

Lynne

DEDICATION

For all the spouses and families who are patiently waiting for their soldiers to return home.

As always, for T.S., my real life hero.

CHAPTER 1

Navy SEAL Ryan McLaughlin pulled opened the wooden door of the Ready Room, his team's favorite hangout, and stepped into the dimly lit bar. Breathing a sigh of relief that they'd made it back in one piece, he inhaled the familiar scents of fried food and beer. As usual, he was the first to arrive, and he grabbed their regular table in the back.

A few moments later, Pam, their regular server, showed up with two pitchers of Dogfish Head Pale Ale and five frosted mugs. It was a testament to how often they hung out there, that she knew their order.

"Welcome back, Ryan. Tough one?"

"Yeah, you could say that." She knew they

were SEALs and that was as much as she'd ask. Most of the clientele were service members since it was located near Naval Air Station Oceana, Norfolk Naval Station, JEB Fort Story, and the Dam Neck Annex. If you threw a dart, you'd hit a service member.

"I'll be back to check on you in a bit."

"Thanks." Now, he needed the rest of the team to arrive. The Ready Room was a post mission tradition. If it was during business hours, the team met for a few beers and unwound before heading home. Ryan was glad that so far it hadn't changed since Rafe and Cam had settled down. Some traditions needed to be kept.

Rolling his shoulders to ease some of the built up tension, Ryan closed his eyes and went over the last three weeks. It was FUBAR. They'd barely made it out of Syria with their asses still attached. There had been more than the usual close calls. At least they'd gotten the package, a Russian chemist, who'd been held hostage by the new ISIS-Al-Qaeda group. Ryan almost felt sorry for the guy. His debriefing wouldn't be fun. The CIA wasn't known for their gentleness especially when they didn't know which side of the fence their HVT stood.

"Do you want me to take the mugs back to the freezer?" Pam asked.

"They should be here any second now." He'd barely answered her when sunlight poured in as the bar's door opened. The guys had picked up a straggler. "Looks like we'll need another mug. Can you bring an order of the loaded nachos too?"

"You got it," she said after looking over her shoulder at the rest of the team. "Be right back with everything."

"Hey Pam, how's it going?" Rafe asked as he sat at the table. Rafe Buchanan was number two on the team and their best sniper. He'd been with his girlfriend, Meghan, almost since they'd met in the Norfolk Airport last year. It was one of those fairy tale kind of meetings. Then they went through hell before she moved to Norfolk and they moved in together.

Ryan was happy for them, but relationships weren't for him. "What took you jokers so long? I thought I was going to have to drink these by myself."

Murph laughed as he pulled out a chair and

sat down, then tilted his head over his shoulder. "We found this deadbeat hanging out in the parking lot." Drew "Murph" Murphy was the ballistics guy. You wouldn't find anyone who loved blowing things up more than he did. If they needed to break the tension, Murph was *the* guy. It didn't matter what the situation, he'd find a way to make a joke and attract any lady within earshot.

The extra man with his team was Matthew "Wolf" Steel. Wolf's team was notorious around NAS Oceana and throughout the spec ops community. It was the reason they knew John "Tex" Keegan, a computer guru they'd tapped more than a few times to help with intel. "Slumming, Wolf?" Ryan asked as he shook his hand.

"You're not going to believe this, but I'm on vacation."

"I don't. Why here? You couldn't come up with a more exotic destination?" Jake remarked. Master Chief Jake Warner was the "boss" of the Black Eagle Team and the oldest, not that you'd be able to tell. He worked harder than any of them. The only reason anyone would know at all were the gray hairs showed up on his temples a few months ago.

"Caroline has wanted to go on a cruise for ages. I finally was able to book one. Then after we got here, we found out there was a problem with the ship."

"What kind of issue?" Rafe asked.

"On their return trip a fire broke out in the engine room. They stopped in Puerto Rico for the passengers to disembark and allow them to inspect the ship to determine the status. After I heard about it, I contacted a friend in the Coasties, but that was all he could tell me."

"Fuck, that sucks."

"Yeah. Caroline said I'd arranged it so I wouldn't have to go."

"I totally get that," Ryan replied. Frogmen had their fill of boats on missions. It wouldn't be his first or even sixth choice for a vacation.

"So where's Caroline?" Jake asked.

"One of the women she used to work with lives in Williamsburg and just had a baby. Since we're stuck here for who knows how long, she went to visit her. I came over here hoping to see some familiar faces."

"You got lucky. We just got back a couple of hours ago," Ryan said.

"Yeah, that's what Jake said. Rough one from

the looks of you guys."

"Seems to be the norm lately," Jake replied.

"Ain't that the truth. The shit is getting worse instead of better."

Pam appeared behind Jake and put the extra mug and a huge tray of nachos on the table. Then she leaned below the table to say 'hi' to Halo and set down a bowl of water and some doggy snacks for him. "Anyone need anything else?"

"I think we're good."

"Just holler if you do."

"Thanks, Pam. You're the best," Cam said as he filled the mugs with the frosty brew.

"I know," Pam answered with a huge smile and a wink. She'd been working at the Ready Room for as long as any of them could remember. In her late fifties, she was a staple at the bar.

Cameron "Cam" Patterson was the youngest member of the Black Eagles. He'd joined them about five years ago and was the K-9 handler. He and Halo were so in sync it was scary, and the dog followed him everywhere. Cam met his girlfriend, Miranda Stanhope, when the team rescued her and her missionary group from the Taliban.

The so-called mastermind behind the abduction was the only one who'd gotten away. Tex was trying to locate him for them, but the stars would have to align just right for their team to be the one to get him. Azfaar's plotting had nearly killed Miranda and Cam on US soil. As long as he lived or was on the run, their team and their women weren't safe. Ryan hated that they had to follow the "rules" even though the jihadists out to destroy America didn't have the same restrictions.

After all the mugs were full, Jake lifted his and the others followed. "To absent brothers."

"To absent brothers," they echoed.

Ryan sighed with pleasure as the first swallow of the icy brew slid down his throat. There was nothing like the flavor of his favorite draft. A little more of his tension eased as his body realized he was home. Then his stomach growled, reminding him it had been over twenty-four hours since he'd eaten.

Picking up a loaded chip, he popped it into his mouth. It was like manna from heaven. For the next few minutes they dug into the nachos, only stopping long enough to refill their glasses.

The expression on their faces mirrored Ryan's. They could relax, at least for now. When they'd gotten on the transport he'd had a beer and went to sleep. It was phase one of his decompression, but he never really relaxed until he was back in the US.

"Haven't eaten lately?" Wolf asked.

"I can't even remember the last MRE. The whole mission was a real clusterfuck," Ryan responded as soon as he'd swallowed the food in his mouth. His mother had raised him right.

"It was," Jake agreed. "I don't know how it's been with for your team, but things have gone down the shitter over the last year. Each mission is worse than the one before with bad or no intel. They need to hire Tex, then maybe things wouldn't be so fucked up."

"I agree. It's been the same for us," Wolf said.

"Our CIA Liaison got burned about six months ago. Not sure how things got so fucked but he's been sidelined. We were lucky an FBI analyst bailed us out when one our HVTs who'd evaded capture sent his crew after us here."

"The FBI got involved? How did that work? We can't operate on home soil," Wolf asked.

"We weren't technically operating here. They ran point and she kept us in the loop with her boss's permission. The analyst is also Meghan's best friend. They grew up in Atlanta together," Rafe answered.

"Meghan's your woman, right?"

"Yeah."

"I heard rumors about that mission. I thought me and Caroline had a helluva story, but yours was pretty fucked up too."

"It's weird how things work out. We rescued Miranda Stanhope on the same mission and now she's dating Cam."

"Really? A twofer? Congrats, bro."

"Thanks," Cam responded in between bites.

"Who's next? Murph, Ryan, or you Jake?"

"Fuck no," Murph and Ryan answered in unison and then laughed when they heard themselves. Jake remained silent and Ryan wondered if he was involved with someone they didn't know about. He never had shared anything about his personal life.

"I like women too much to settle down," Murph said before he stuffed another loaded chip into his mouth.

"That's not the whole truth. We bet he'd be hooked up within two years. He's just about through the first year. But when he loses, he'll be serving beer in a pink tutu during the first charity event they have here."

"How did you get roped into that," Wolf asked.

"If, not when. I wouldn't be holding your breath, either. You're all a bunch of assclowns if you think I'll get chained to a woman. I took the bet because it's easy money for the charity, it's a sure thing."

"A sure thing doesn't exist. Hell, you should know that by now, frogman," Jake said.

"He's right," Wolf said. "Do you have the same bet, Ryan?"

"Nope."

"That's it, just nope?"

"Yup," Ryan answered as he downed what was left of his beer.

"He's interested in someone, but he's fighting it hard," Rafe said. So much for secrets between friends. Ryan mentioned to Rafe once that if he was going to date anyone it would be someone like Chrissy. He'd expected it to stay between them. "He likes Chrissy, Meghan's friend."

"The FBI agent?"

"Yup."

"You need to keep your trap shut, dickhead. I never said that."

"Seems like someone protests too much," Murph said. Leave it to him to butt in. "Aww, look, he's pouting."

Ryan growled and his chair scraped on the floor as he pushed away from the table. He'd show Murph who was pouting. Jake's hand on his arm stopped him. Damn, he didn't want to deal with this shit. When did downtime get so fucked up? "Can we drop it now?"

Seeing movement out of the corner of his eye he tensed, but it was Halo. After giving him big puppy dog eyes, he laid his head on Ryan's knee. His stress must have been evident enough for the dog to pick up on it.

"Sorry, bro, I didn't realize it was a touchy subject," Wolf said.

"No worries. I'm sorry, too. I don't know why I'm so tense."

"We all are," Jake said. His eyes were filled with compassion as they met Ryan's. He knew more of Ryan's story than anyone else, even though he was closest to Rafe. Jake saw his records and psych eval when he picked him for the Black Eagle team seven years earlier. They'd never discussed it, and he wondered if that was about to change.

Chrissy Stillwell tapped on the office door of Special Agent in Charge Brent Pierson, her boss and the Middle East section chief. After combing through intel briefs for hours and pulling the new reports that had been filed overnight, it was time to share her concerns.

SAC Pierson wasn't much older than Chrissy, with dark brown hair and deep brown eyes, under different circumstances she might have been attracted to him. He was a fair boss, but everything always had to be by the book, all "t's" crossed and "i's" dotted. "Come in, Chrissy. What's up?" Pierson took off his glasses and closed the folder in front of him before giving her his full attention.

"I was going through last night's intel. The report of a fire in the engine room of the Jewel, one of the Island Sun cruise ships, jumped out at me."

"What's so special about the fire?"

"Nothing, if it was just one. But I've been

following intel on this cruise line for the last six months. The Coast Guard has reports of other fires, engine issues, employee illnesses, all on ships from this cruise line. It was happening about once a month. That was weird, but over the last two months, it's been happening almost every cruise."

"How did you get intel for the Caribbean? It's not our section."

"I was trying to figure out the reason we were getting reports of all the new jihadists cells popping up. So I asked to see the shipping information for the Atlantic."

"Another one of your hunches?"

Chrissy tried hard not to flinch under his piercing stare. He'd told her before she could follow her gut as long as she didn't go to him until she had proof to back up her speculations. "Well, yeah. The cruise line is based in Turkey. No, I'm not profiling, but would it be that hard to check it out to see if I'm right?"

Pierson's silence made her antsy. This job was important to her and she didn't want to do anything to put it in jeopardy. But her hunches had been right every time over the last three years. Enough that she had to trust them. Finally, he grabbed a pen and made some notes then met her eyes.

"Tell me what you know."

Opening the folder in her hand, she pulled out a copy of her report and slid it across his desk. It was so shiny he probably kept a can of Pledge stashed away. She even detected the faint scent of the lemon polish. A weird thought to pop into her head but it was the way her brain worked always flying off on tangents triggered by the smallest detail. But that's why the CIA tried to recruit her in college. Turning them down, she chose the FBI instead, wanting to help keep her country safe.

As her boss followed along, she described the most recent incidents that occurred on the ships from Island Sun cruise lines. Each time they were forced to make emergency stops in Puerto Rico and offload the passengers.

"Why do you think it's Puerto Rico?"

"I wasn't sure at first, but if they're smuggling people and possibly weapons, the security would be less stringent since it's US soil."

He nodded. "You think these are related? It couldn't just be a run of bad luck? Or maybe it's sabotage from disgruntled employees?"

"I checked into the company. There haven't been any labor disputes reported. They aren't a huge cruise line and only started sailing out of the Port in Norfolk a year ago. Why go from a local cruise line sailing in the Mediterranean to sailing the Caribbean? It's too much of a coincidence."

"I agree. Do a deep dive into the company. I want to know everything there is to know about the Island Sun Cruise Line and the owners. If we have to get the NSA involved we will. But they had to file papers and get cleared to sail from the port."

"Yes, sir."

"I'll bring this up at our status meeting this afternoon. Get me anything new before then."

"Will do."

"We'll see where this goes. But after you untangled the mess with that SEAL team, I am learning to trust your hunches too."

"Thank you, sir." Chrissy stood up, nodded briefly to her boss, and then hurried back to her desk. Now that she'd been given the official go ahead she'd have more leeway and could get assistance from other analysts if she needed help. There was definitely something weird with those ships and she was determined to find out.

Navigating through cube-land, she was already coming up with options and possible theories, then discarding them almost as quickly. Her bestie, Meghan, was one of the few people who knew how her mind worked and that she had an eidetic memory.

It wasn't until high school that she'd figured out how different she was from most people. Until then, she'd assumed everyone thought the same way. But when she kept acing exam after exam without any apparent effort they'd gotten approval from her parents to do some testing. It turned high school into a miserable disaster. Word got out and the kids gave her grief and mostly avoided her. Except for Meghan.

Their friendship had never changed from the day they'd met. Meghan didn't give a crap if she acted differently at times. Chrissy doubted she'd care if she was an alien trying to steal their brains. The thought made her giggle, and she laughed harder when her phone vibrated in her desk drawer a moment later. Of course it was Meghan.

"Hey girl. What's up?"

"You sound happy," Meghan said in her soft southern drawl. She'd worked hard to lose it, but Chrissy always heard it.

"I was thinking about you and laughing when you called. Mind reading?"

"Nah, just good timing, I guess. Are you busy tonight?"

"Planning a Girl's Night?"

"Not this time. Rafe got back this morning. I thought I'd have everyone over for some pizza. Can you make it?"

"Everyone?"

"Yes Ryan will be there, at least I think he will. But there will also be another couple there. He's on the teams and based in Coronado."

Chrissy looked at the new stack of paperwork that appeared on her desk while she was in with Pierson. "What time should I be there?"

"Does six thirty work for you?"

"Yup that should work, unless I get caught in traffic. Want me to bring anything?"

"Nope, I've got it covered. You've been so busy, I miss you."

"I know. Sorry. Actually, I wish it was just us girls. One of these days I'm going to rip Mr. Pissy Pants a new one if he doesn't let up."

"He doesn't mean anything by it."

"Maybe. Jury's out on that one. And Murph? I'm going to laugh my ass off when a woman finally shows him what life is really like."

"Right? Oh my God, I'd kill to see that happen."

"Okay, let me go. I've got a ton of work to get through before I can get out of here on time."

"See you later."

Murph was a pain in the ass with his constant flirting but at least when he was there he kept her mind off Ryan. He was the real trouble. The first time she'd met him, she couldn't swallow, and her heart almost beat out of her chest. It was like some kind of romance out of a movie, except it wasn't. Closing her eyes as she pictured Ryan, his face came into focus like a photograph. From his emerald green eyes, shaggy auburn hair, and his perfect two-day beard. It didn't matter when she saw him, it was always just the same.

"Ugh, snap out of it, woman," she whispered to herself. She had work to do and daydreaming about Mr. Tall, Dark, and Pissy wouldn't help her get it done.

CHAPTER 2

Ryan recognized Cam and Jake's trucks as he searched the parking lot in Rafe's complex for a spot. What he didn't see was Chrissy's Jeep. Maybe she wouldn't make it. As he grabbed the two six-packs of beer he'd bought, he wondered if he was relieved or disappointed.

It was almost guaranteed that she was there when he was. He still hadn't figured out if Meghan and Rafe had planned it that way. From the vibes he'd picked up from her, she wasn't interested in dating him anymore than he was in her. Although, it was a lie. He was plenty interested. "Fuck."

"What's wrong, froggy?" That answered his

question. How she'd snuck up on him he had no idea.

"Hey, Chrissy. I didn't know if you were going to be here or not."

"Don't you mean that you were hoping I wouldn't show up?"

"No..."

"I call bullshit."

Ryan sighed. She read him like a book. It surprised him he'd managed to keep his attraction hidden from her. But tonight he was tired, mentally and physically. The last thing he wanted to do was spar with her all evening. "Okay, so maybe a little. How about we call a truce for tonight? I'm beat."

For a second he swore compassion flashed in her big brown eyes. He could sink into them forever, but he couldn't, or maybe it was wouldn't.

"Sure, froggy. I'll go easy on you tonight," she answered with her crooked grin. She wasn't beautiful in the usual sense, but her dark eyes and blonde hair, and sharp cheekbones created a striking vision he couldn't get out of his head.

"Thanks," he responded with a grin. It was odd, but whatever tension he'd still been hauling around with him drained onto the asphalt with her smile. Damn, he had it worse than he thought.

"Rougher than usual?" Chrissy asked as she walked with him toward Rafe's apartment.

"It was a total cluster fuck." She nodded at his response but didn't say anything.

Her response made Ryan wonder if she'd heard any chatter about the uptick in activity. But he couldn't ask her any more than she could ask him.

Meghan opened the door as Chrissy reached out to knock. She looked at each of them and smiled. "Glad you both made it. Everyone else is here."

"Sorry, the tunnel was backed up," Chrissy said as she followed Meghan into the apartment. Rafe couldn't stop himself from watching her ass in the tight blue jeans. The woman packed some major curves.

"Are you coming inside, Ryan? Or are you just going to stand in the doorway all night?" Meghan asked with a wink. She'd earned the right to tease him after what she'd gone through before they'd rescued her. She was every bit the spitfire Rafe called her. He hadn't thought there was someone feistier until he'd met Chrissy. Talk about a little hellion. Holy shit.

Closing the door behind him, he stepped into the crowded apartment. This pizza get together had become a homecoming tradition since Meghan moved in with Rafe. They all showed up with beer usually, and Cam brought Halo and Miranda who brought dessert. Rafe invited Wolf and Caroline since they were in town with nothing to do.

"About time you got your happy ass here. I was getting ready to send out a search party," Rafe said as he pounded him on the back. Then under his breath he asked, "Everything okay?"

"Yeah, why?"

"You walked in with Chrissy and you weren't fighting," Rafe said with a huge grin. "I thought you might have gotten banged on the head when I wasn't looking."

"Asshole. We called a truce for tonight."

"Really? That's interesting."

"No, it isn't. Drop it," Ryan said with a low growl.

"Okay, geesh, don't go animal on me."

"It's only a heartbeat away. Don't poke the bear." But as he answered, Ryan softened his voice and smiled. Maybe it was time for some leave. He couldn't remember the last time he'd taken R and R.

"C'mon, you need a beer and a slice. Have you met Caroline yet?"

"Not yet." He grabbed a beer, handed the rest to Rafe then joined the group of men who'd become family. They were sitting around the coffee table that was covered end to end with pizza boxes.

"About time, bro," Murph said and indicated a spot next to him on the floor. He kept his eyeroll to himself and plastered what he'd hoped was a smile on his face.

"This is from someone who's never on time to anything?"

"I was tonight."

"Yeah, because there's free food and beer. I guess I should adjust that to *unless* there is a free meal involved."

"I can't argue with that," Murph said with a huge grin.

Wolf stood up and shook Ryan's hand again. "This is my wife, Caroline."

"Nice to meet you. I've heard a lot about you. I'm Ryan, the brilliant one in this group." That elicited lots of, "yeah rights" from his team mates.

He'd been warned that she was reserved, but when she smiled it lit up her whole face. "It's nice to meet you too. Listening to you guys is like being around Matthew's team."

"It happens when you spend so much time around each other," Jake said.

"Yes, exactly."

"Yup, we're one big family," Murph commented.

"Thank God one woman didn't give birth to y'all. She'd have run for the hills," Chrissy said as she followed Meghan into the room. "Hi, I'm Chrissy."

"Nice to meet you," Caroline said with a smile.

"Geesh, Chrissy, way to make an entrance, girlfriend," Meghan said with a laugh.

"Just sayin it like it is, and y'all know it too." Her look dared them to disagree. It was one of the things Ryan admired most about her. She always said what she was thinking, good or bad. But damn did it stir up trouble sometimes.

"I've thought that about Matthew's team too.

They manage to get themselves into lots of trouble."

"Hey, that's not fair. It's usually when we have to save our women," Wolf replied and pulled Caroline closer against her side.

Their story was well-known throughout spec ops. If it weren't for Caroline, Wolf's team would have been taken out by terrorists, and that would have only been the beginning. She was a true hero.

Ryan grabbed a paper plate and a slice of pepperoni pizza and handed it to Chrissy who'd taken the only open spot left open around the table—next to him. Karma really was a bitch. The universe was determined to keep throwing them together.

"Thanks, but what if I didn't want pepperoni?"

"You always eat pepperoni."

"Observant for someone who doesn't like me."

"It's my job, woman. Besides, I never said I didn't like you." This conversation needed to stop before it headed into deeper waters he wasn't ready to navigate. Turning to Caroline, he asked, "Wolf said you were supposed to be on a cruise?"

"Yes. I'd been looking forward to it for months. Matthew surprised me with the tickets for my birthday. But when we arrived the ship hadn't returned to port yet. Some problem with the engine, I think."

"An engine fire actually," Wolf interjected. "They had to dock in Puerto Rico to check the ship."

"Damn, that sucks."

"Wait, did you say an engine fire? It wasn't an Island Sun cruise was it?" Chrissy interrupted.

"Yes, it was. Why?" Wolf asked.

Chrissy didn't answer at first, and Ryan could almost see her calculating what she could and couldn't say. It was fascinating to watch.

"You never heard this from me, but you could dig up some interesting information from the Coast Guard reports. I'd look back over the last year and see what you find."

Wolf and Jake nodded in sync and Ryan went from being fascinated to wondering what she'd discovered. He didn't doubt for a second that she was on to something. After watching her unravel all the crap with Azfaar, he'd trust her with his life or more importantly his team's lives.

The wheels turned in Chrissy's mind as she analyzed the new data and sifted it into what she already knew. Would it be possible to have Wolf and Caroline do some undercover work on their cruise, if they got on the ship? She wasn't sure how much leave he had available. He probably wouldn't want to use time with his wife to go undercover.

It would be dangerous, and Caroline was a civilian, so it would have to be off books. It was happening too often lately, this skirting on the edge of the law. But it might help her confirm her suspicions if he could dig up anything.

"Can you say anything else?" Jake asked.

"Just check the Coast Guard reports."

"I thought you were assigned to the Middle East section?" Meghan asked as she lifted her glass of wine to take a sip.

"I am, but I got a hunch." Meghan nodded. Chrissy knew Meghan would understand what she meant. She could also count on her not to out her "weirdness" to the team. They guys were great, but she'd been burned too many times.

"We got a text that the ship would be back in port tomorrow. They'll depart the day after. It said they'll give everyone a partial refund since they have to shorten the cruise by two days," Caroline said.

"I'm not sure we should go," Wolf said. "What do you think, Chrissy?"

"I don't think y'all would be in danger. I didn't mean to ruin your vacation."

"You didn't. We're used to this. Trouble follows Matthew everywhere he goes," Caroline said with a smile.

"I have an idea, but I need to run it up the food chain first. Can I have Jake contact you?"

"Sure is. Thanks," Wolf said. "I have a buddy in the Coasties. I'll give him a call."

"We could give Tex a call too," Jake added. "It's not that late."

"Good idea."

Way to go, Chrissy. Nothing like throwing a wet blanket over the evening and their vacation. Social interactions were so hard for her. She'd gotten better mostly because Meghan helped her out of so many awkward situations. It was the main reason she was happy to work at the FBI and come home to her cat, Enigma. All of her relationships ended in disaster. It was so damn hard for her to let her guard down that she couldn't fully commit to anyone and it would always catch up with her.

"This is supposed to be time to relax and celebrate that you're back home, not plotting another mission," Miranda, Cam's girlfriend said.

"She's right, I didn't mean to screw up the party." Chrissy fought the urge to cut and run for the door.

"You didn't, Chrissy. One thing led to another. That's all," Ryan said. His usual hard emerald eyes were softer and filled with compassion. Compassion? The man had never shown her so much as a sliver of anything nice before. What was going on tonight?

Nodding, she took a long swig of her wine. "I think I need a refill."

"Me too," Miranda said.

Rafe refilled all the wine glasses and passed out beers. It gave Chrissy a chance to settle down. She felt Meghan's concern from across the room, but she didn't want to meet her eyes. If she did, she might lose it. Instead, she closed her eyes and took a deep breath. Inhale. Exhale. It had been ages since she'd reacted like this. It might be all the extra hours she'd been putting in, or maybe the new people. Either way, she needed to get a grip.

"You'll be okay. Just keep breathing in and out," Ryan whispered in her ear. His voice so low she wasn't sure he'd really spoken, but his warm breath and the scratch of his beard against her ear made it all too real.

The whole evening was like a trip to bizarro world. Maybe she was really home in bed. Only one way to prove it. Pinching her arm, proved it and Ryan chuckled.

"Why did you do that?" he asked.

"I needed to make sure I wasn't imagining all of this."

"Does that happen often?" Damn. Why had he decided to be nice to her tonight? He'd either been rude or avoided her most since they'd met. Was the universe playing tricks on her? Because it sure seemed like it.

"No, not really. It's just a weird evening, like one of those backwards days they had in school. You know?"

"We didn't have those, or I don't remember them if we did."

Thankful for something...anything to talk about besides her, she explained how it worked.

"I used to love those," Miranda said.

"Me too. Chrissy and I would plan what we were going to wear weeks ahead of time," Meghan added.

"How long have you known each other?" Caroline asked.

"Since elementary school. But we've been besties since junior high."

"That's so cool. I never had close friends until I met Matthew and the team."

"Oh dear, that's sad."

"It's all in the past. I love my life. Whatever brought me here was worth the journey."

"Amen to that," Meghan and Miranda said at the same time.

Relief surged through Chrissy as the conversation moved away from her and focused on Caroline. She told them some of shit her friends went through before they found their happiness. They were incredible stories. It seemed like trial by fire was a requirement for a relationship with a frogman. Miranda and Meghan had the same type of story.

"Better?" Rafe asked.

Chrissy had been focused on Caroline's words and seeing the threads of related information and following them, when she heard Ryan's voice.

"Yes, thanks." Maybe the real Ryan was taken by a body snatcher on this last mission, because he sure as well wasn't acting like his normal self. She needed to talk to Meghan and see if something had happened. Maybe he'd gotten hit over the head and had a concussion.

"Good."

It took all she had not to squirm. Staring into his eyes turned her insides into jelly. Ohhh, maybe he was just horny. Or was that just her? "Can I ask you a question?"

"Sure, but I can't promise to give you an answer."

"What's going on with you? Normally you stay as far away from me as possible. If you interact it's usually rude or snarky. So, something has to be up."

"Maybe I'm just tired. Why does something have to be wrong?"

"Because you're ass backward. First the truce, then being nice..."

"Would you rather I ignore you?"

"No, yes, maybe, I don't know. But there has to be a reason you're different. Nothing happens without a reason. Cause and effect."

"I'm sorry if I've seemed rude."

"Not seemed, you've definitely been rude, standoffish and made me feel like you couldn't stand the sight of me." Geesh, Chrissy, maybe that was a little harsh.

"I'll accept that, but it has nothing to do with you. I'm sorry if I made you feel bad."

"Okay, I'll accept your apology. Does this mean it'll be different from now on?"

"I can't promise I won't backslide, but I will make a concerted effort."

Chrissy nodded. Maybe she'd fallen down a rabbit hole after she'd gotten out of the Jeep. But nice Ryan would be a lot harder to keep at arm's length than asshat Ryan.

For the first time, she and Ryan actually chatted. He'd been so uptight every time they'd been around each other, it was nice to see the "real" Ryan. The one everyone else saw. At one point, she looked up and saw Meghan watching them with a smile. Chrissy wondered how long it would take her friend to call her once she left that evening. The phone would probably be ringing before she got to the car.

Chrissy enjoyed talking to Ryan and learning a bit about him. She could listen to his voice for hours, it was deep with just the slightest accent, but she couldn't figure it out. He didn't talk about his family and shared some stories about the team. When he told her about the bet they made with Murph, she lost it. Imagining him walking around the Ready Room in a pink tutu was freaking hysterical.

"Yeah, right? He's made it through the first year though. If he keeps this up we'll be out of luck," Ryan said.

"You just need to throw the right woman in his path. Everyone falls for someone."

"Do you really believe that?"

"I do. It may not happen when we want it to, but, yup, I do."

"I'm not so sure."

"I'm not saying it's always perfect or has a happily ever after, this *is* the real world. But I do believe there is someone for everyone."

Ryan seemed to consider what she'd said and nodded. "I guess time will tell."

The hurt in his eyes made her wonder if he'd had his heart broken. Chrissy avoided relationships and had never been in love. But it didn't stop her from believing that true love existed. Her parents were the first ones to show her, and Meghan and Rafe had it in spades. Yeah, her true love was out there, maybe closer than she wanted to admit.

CHAPTER 3

The party broke up shortly before ten. It was earlier than usual, but they were all wiped out from the mission. It was as if once they got home the adrenaline dissipated like air escaping from a balloon. Ryan was ready for about ten hours of sleep but wanted to talk to Rafe alone before he left. Unfortunately, but it didn't quite work out as he'd hoped since Jake, Wolf, and Caroline were still chatting.

"What's going on?" Ryan asked after Caroline followed Meghan into the kitchen with the leftovers.

"I messaged Tex earlier. He just got back to me. Looks like Chrissy found something interesting," Jake said.

"How does he know what she found? Is he hacking the FBI now?"

"No, but he did take a peek at the Coast Guard reports from the last year," Wolf answered.

"Remind me not to get on his bad side."

"No shit," Jake added. "So what's the deal? Are the ships just pieces of shit or what?"

"It looks like something else. The Island Sun cruise line didn't even exist two years ago. The company showed up out of nowhere with a home port registered as Turkey. Last year they filed the paperwork to sail from Norfolk."

"Okay, maybe a little weird, but I'm still not seeing a problem other than poor maintenance. Why would it trigger an FBI investigation?" Ryan asked, thinking that he should have just gone home.

"Tex is looking deeper, but there are an inordinate amount of stops in Puerto Rico, which is not on any of their itineraries. And it's happening more frequently over the last few months. It's American soil and they aren't as diligent with security monitoring of the passengers and crew," Jake replied.

"What are we thinking? Smuggling? Or something worse?"

"That's probably why Chrissy is investigating if I had to take a guess. But she can't share with us any more than we could share with her. I'm surprised she said as much as she did," Wolf commented.

"But she covered her ass," Rafe said. "There shouldn't be any blowback on her. But you think it's bigger than smuggling don't you?"

Jake nodded. "Tex thinks they're bringing in jihadists or weapons or both. It makes the most sense with all the new terror cells springing up all over. They could get off in Puerto Rico without having to go through customs and take a plane or small boat to the US carrying in just about anything."

"Fucking hell," Ryan said with a low whistle. What a fucking mess, thank God Chrissy was an analyst and not in the field. If what Jake and Tex thought was true, this was going to be a huge operation and bound to be messy.

"What's going on?" Meghan asked. They turned to see the women standing in the doorway. Ryan wondered how long they'd been standing there.

"Nothing yet," Rafe answered. Ryan admired how she never gave Rafe any shit when he couldn't share. It wasn't easy being involved with a special operator, always so many secrets to keep. Lots of women felt shut out. Ryan had seen more than his share of divorces over the years.

"From the look on your faces, I don't think we're going on a cruise. Are we?" Caroline asked as she leaned into Wolf.

"I'm not sure yet. But it's not looking great, no. I'll make it up to you."

"I know." She smiled. "I'm getting tired. We need to figure out where we're staying tonight."

"You're welcome to stay here. We have a guest room," Meghan offered.

Wolf and Caroline exchanged glances. It was as if they knew what the other was thinking without having to say a word. How did Wolf deal with leaving her behind knowing there was a chance he wouldn't return? He'd asked Rafe once, but all he'd said is that Meghan knew the risks. The answer didn't cut it. Ryan saw what it did to a woman when she was left to pick up the pieces.

"We'd love to, if it's not an imposition," Caroline said.

"None at all. It'll give me a chance to get to know you better and you can share some tricks on how to deal with the long deployments," Meghan said as she led Caroline down the hallway to the guest room.

"I guess that's settled." Wolf grinned. "Are you sure you don't mind, Rafe?"

"Nope. Not at all. Although Caroline doesn't know what she's in for. Meghan won't stop plying her with questions."

"Caroline can handle it. She's kept all our women sane as they got involved with the guys. I still can't believe my luck in finding her."

"And you don't worry about the 'what ifs'?"

"No, we've talked about it more than once. We worry about each other, but it's my life. I do what I can to stay safe, we all do, but you can't stop living because you're worried about what could happen."

"Maybe..." Ryan needed some sleep. From the moment he'd seen Chrissy he'd felt off balance. Being around her made him think about possibilities he'd decided against long ago. It was a moment of weakness he couldn't afford.

"When you find the woman of your dreams you'll feel differently. Why give up one moment of happiness worrying about something that may never happen? Live for the moment, not the long term. We knew that when we chose to join the teams."

"I'm happy for you, both of you."

"If you let down your walls, you'd see. Chrissy would go out with you in a heartbeat if you asked her," Rafe said.

"Bullshit. The only reason we got along tonight is because we decided on a temporary truce. We'll be back to arguing the next time we're together, you'll see."

"Ryan, I know you don't know me well, but I'll tell you what I told my guys. If you have feelings for a woman you'd be crazy to deny them. Life is too short and has no guarantees. Don't blow your chance at happiness."

"I hear you. I do. But I have my reasons."

Wolf nodded. Ryan was sorry he'd opened up this can of worms.

"Wolf, are you going to cancel the cruise?" Jake asked.

"I don't know. I don't like the idea of putting Caroline in danger. But from what Tex said the passengers haven't been involved. I am curious what they're up to."

"Maybe we'll get more intel in the morning. Although, if it's the FBI's baby, I'm not sure we'll be read in."

"It could end up being a joint operation since the ships are in international waters."

"It'd be a switch from dropping into the middle of Syria to extract another fucktard," Rafe said.

Ryan agreed with him. He'd had a bad feeling about the HVT on their last mission. The chemist made his gut twist the moment he saw him. Something about the guy didn't seem right. He'd half expected him to pull out a grenade and blow them to bits.

"Alright, I'm heading home. I hope to see you again before you leave. It was great meeting the infamous Wolf."

"That's so much shit. There is nothing infamous about me, except my wife," he said with a grin as Caroline and Meghan returned.

"It was nice meeting you, Caroline. Rafe, you going to join me for a run in the morning?"

"Doubtful, but we'll see."

Ryan nodded and winked at Meghan.

In the parking lot, he walked around his truck then checked underneath for explosive ordinance. It was all about situational awareness and second nature for all of them since Cam's attack and Miranda's kidnapping.

Azfaar made him think about Chrissy. Had she gotten home safe? Her assistance with that mission put her in as much shit as them. Before he realized, he'd turned toward her condo. Just a quick check to make sure she was safe couldn't hurt and no one would have to know. Then he'd go home and some sleep for the first time in weeks.

He pulled into a spot across the street and parked. The lights were on inside and her Jeep was parked in the lot. Relief washed over him, his hellion was home safe and sound. At least for now. But as he sat with the engine rumbling, he couldn't help but wonder what trouble this mess would get her into.

After a few moments, he put his truck in gear and headed home. Hopefully, after a sleeping in his own bed, he'd be back to normal in the morning. Then he could put all these thoughts out of his head for good.

Chrissy couldn't relax after she got back home. Between thinking about Ryan and the cruise line, her brain wouldn't shut down. Typical, but sometimes she just wanted to shut her brain down. But once she got an idea she couldn't let it go until it was solved. Ryan seemed different at the party, vulnerable, which never happened.

Meghan said he never took time off. If the team had down time he'd spend it doing PT and volunteering at the local Boys & Girls Club. She sighed with exasperation and shook her head to remove thoughts of Ryan from her mind. For now, she needed to focus on the Island Sun Cruise Line. It sounded like a Nancy Drew story, but if she was correct, it was no children's story.

Her mind made up, she showered, dressed and went into work. Security wouldn't be surprised, this happened whenever she had a puzzle to solve. What she hadn't expected was her phone to ring as she drove to her office in Chesapeake. Upgrading the stereo and adding the hands free shit to her Jeep was the only change she made since she bought it five years ago. It was her baby and she wanted to keep it as original as possible.

Clicking the button on the dash, she answered.

"Hey Meghan, I figured you and Rafe would be busy by now."

"Wolf and Caroline are staying the night."

"Well fuck me running, no hanky-panky for you, huh?"

"I didn't say that," Meghan said with a giggle. Chrissy grinned, just talking about sex turned Meghan into a giddy school girl.

"Did something happen after I left?"

"No, maybe? I'm not sure. You know the guys. But Tex is looking into the cruise line now. But that's not why I'm calling."

Chrissy's attention sharpened as soon as Meghan mentioned Tex's name. What had he dug up? John "Tex" Keegan could locate information better than almost anyone. She'd like to think she could give him a run for his money, but he didn't have to follow the same rules she did.

"Chrissy. Are you listening?"

"Sorry. I'm driving."

"What? Where the hell are you going? It's eleven thirty."

"Yes, it is. Wow. We can both tell time. Imagine that."

"Don't evade. You're going back to work? Damn it. You need to rest. You looked as bad as the guys tonight. When was the last time you slept?"

"I don't know. You know how I get when I'm working on something."

"Yes, I do. And that's why I called. You weren't yourself tonight. And what was up with you and Ryan? Did you finally decide to give in to your mutual attraction?"

"Nothing and no. We declared a one evening truce. I think he's worn out. Jake should make him take some leave. The guy looks burned out."

"I know. But he won't. And they're SEALs. I was told that's not how they operate."

"Figures. God forbid they take care of themselves while they save the world."

"More evading. What is going on with you?"

"Nothing. Seriously. I just need to figure this out. It was a mistake to mention it, but when Wolf and Caroline mentioned the cruise ship it took me by surprise."

"You know, speaking of vacation…"

"Don't start. I sit in an office at a computer, I'm fine."

"You know what I mean. Remember what happened when you were at Quantico."

"I'll never forget. It almost cost me my chance."

"Exactly, so please take care of yourself."

"I will. I promise. I'll call you tomorrow. I'm at work."

"Okay, love you."

"Love you too. Give Rafe a kiss for me," Chrissy said with a chuckle as she disconnected the phone. Grabbing her badge, she held it in front of the scanner and waited for the gates to open. The parking lot was almost empty, and she pulled into the first non-reserved spot.

The building was quiet as she walked up the stairs to the second floor and navigated the cube farm to get to her assigned space. Over the last three years, she'd made it her home away from home, with pictures of her and Meghan, and an assortment of Rubik's cubes that helped her when she needed to focus.

After booting her computer, she headed to the breakroom to make a pot of coffee. It was part of her process. Maintaining her routine was better for everyone. The one time she'd gone off track had been a disaster and was the reason

Meghan was worried. But she'd learned her lesson and did what she needed to do to ensure it didn't happen again.

Grabbing a mug, she added two sugars, a splash of half and half and filled it to the rim with coffee. After a couple of sips to make sure it was low enough that she could walk without spilling it, she headed to work.

Chrissy spent the next eight hours poring through files looking for bits and pieces of the puzzle. There were no doubts in her mind that the so-called accidents were created as cover for something or someone. Whether it was to smuggle in people, weapons, or both was the question.

More intel came in overnight on the cruise line and she added it to her files. The connection was there somewhere. But even after three pots of coffee, she hadn't found the one thread to pull it all together. One piece was missing and there was only one way to find it.

CHAPTER 4

By the time Brent Pierson got into the office at seven-thirty, Chrissy had worked up a proposal to find her missing piece. It would be a hard sell, but she had to try. To say she was invested in figuring this out was an understatement.

"Did you spend the night here? I thought we discussed this, Chrissy," Pierson said as he stopped at her cube on the way to his office.

"I know, sir. But I couldn't stop thinking that we were missing something."

"And did you find it?"

"No, not yet."

"Go home, get some sleep." Pierson shook his head and continued on to his office with Chrissy following.

"I'm fine. I am. But I have an idea. I just need to get on one of the ships…"

"We've discussed this. You're not a field agent."

"But I trained as one, I have the credentials, it wasn't my choice to be stuck at a desk."

"You're here because you have a brilliant mind that can find the smallest piece and unravel it. You've saved hundreds maybe thousands of people. That's not a skill to be risked."

"But, sir, I know I can figure it out if I'm there. None of the passengers have been involved, it's the crew that ends up missing when they disembark in Norfolk. How much trouble could I get into?"

Pierson turned around as he unlocked his door with his eyebrows raised. His expression said it all. Okay, maybe she had a reputation of being a bit hot headed when she believed something. But she was right ninety-nine point nine percent of the time. That had to count for something.

"We can put an experienced field agent on the ship to get the intel."

"But I know the details. I'll know what the missing piece is when I see it."

"You can't guarantee that. It's not a puzzle, Chrissy. This is real life where agents are killed in the line of duty all the time. If you're right and these are terrorists we're dealing with, it's too dangerous."

"But.."

"No, unless there is some absolute reason why it has to be you. I'm not putting you on that ship. Get me the rest of your research. I'll talk to the director and see what he says. But I don't want to risk you on this."

"Yes, sir." She needed to back off, for now at least. Maybe the director would take her side. Who was she kidding? How many times had she been told she was too valuable to risk in the field? Still, there had to be a way.

While she waited for the fourth pot of coffee to finish brewing, she came up with the solution. The trick would be to finagle it, so it didn't look like it was her idea. It wouldn't be easy, but she could pull it off, maybe, hopefully.

Pouring two cups of coffee she headed back to her boss's office and knocked on the door.

"I brought you a cup of coffee."

"The answer is still no."

"Right. Have you spoken to the director already?"

"Chrissy…"

"I'm just bringing you coffee and the rest of the intel."

"Thank you. Now I suggest you go home and get some rest." She was going to argue, but what was the point.

"I have a few more files to go through then I'll go home early."

Pierson had been assigned as the SAC just over two years ago after Harold Bradley retired. At first they'd butted heads, but slowly he realized she wasn't trying to usurp his authority, just solve cases.

Nodding, he took the folder from her and turned to his computer. She was dismissed and knew better than to say anything else. Back at her desk, she got to work trying to figure out how to get the SEAL team involved. She could work it in to her notes since the ship was in international waters for most of the time. They'd worked well before, and maybe she could pair up with Rafe and go undercover. They knew each other well enough they wouldn't even have to work at the relationship thing.

It wouldn't be an easy sell. Actually, she couldn't 'sell' it at all. Pierson would have to. Putting the thought in his head would be up to her though. Fiddling with one of her Rubik's cubes, she ran scenarios over and over, discarding one after another, trying to find the one that would work. But just like the missing puzzle piece, she couldn't figure it out other than having it in her notes. It was unlike her. Puzzles were her super power. Maybe Meghan was right, and she needed some time off. If she lost her ability to puzzle solve, it would be like losing part of herself.

In the end, it didn't matter. Once the director was alerted to her suspicions, he authorized Pierson to do whatever it took to uncover what was going on with Island Sun Cruise lines. When he asked her to come to his office, she'd been ready give up and go home.

"Close the door, please." He waited for her to close the door and sit down before he continued. "The director agrees with your assessment and authorized a full investigation of the cruise line including putting someone on board."

As she listened to Pierson describe the operation, she twined her fingers together to keep her excitement in check. When she heard Captain Knox's name she breathed a sigh of relief, maybe the universe was on her side this time.

"Apparently, one of the SEAL team members was supposed to be on the ship that had the latest issue. He proposed sending one of his guys instead and asked if you'd be available as the liaison."

"From here? Or on the ship?"

Pierson looked pained as he answered. "They want you to go undercover with the SEAL as a couple." In her brain she was high-fiving herself and struggled to keep calm.

"Am I going then?"

"I suggested using Agent Carraway, but Knox reminded me that you have an established relationship with the team, and it would work better. Apparently, the director agreed with Captain Knox. So yes, you're going."

"Thank you, sir."

"Don't thank me. If I had my way you'd be staying here. This isn't a game, Chrissy. You need to remember that."

"I will, sir. I realize this is dangerous."

"I've sent the cleared intel to Knox. You need

to go to Little Creek for the mission briefing. I'll be linked in. If you need anything let me know."

"Thank you, sir. I will."

"And Chrissy?"

"Yes, sir?"

"Don't get yourself killed."

"I'll do my best."

With her brain already rushing ahead to the mission briefing, she had to concentrate as she walked to her cubicle. After locking the files in her desk and shutting down the computer, she grabbed her purse and headed for the parking lot.

The sun was shining, and it was hot when Chrissy got into the Jeep. It was mid-September and it didn't look like summer was going anywhere. But it would be perfect cruising weather. Grinning, she clicked on the stereo and blasted her favorite playlist for the twenty minute drive to Joint Expeditionary Base Little Creek-Fort Story, but everyone just called it Little Creek.

In the middle of his ten-mile run on the beach,

Ryan's phone buzzed. It was a text from Jake. The team was supposed to have a few days off, but he'd bet anything that this had something to do with the cruise line Chrissy mentioned last night. Turning around and heading back to his truck. He'd have preferred to go home and grab a shower before reporting, but it wasn't going to happen.

Ryan pulled into the parking lot at Little Creek the same time as Rafe and Murph. Cam's truck was already there and so was Jake's.

"Do you know what this is about?" Ryan asked.

"Nope, just that we needed to report asap," Murph said.

"I haven't heard anything either, but if I had to bet, it has to do with the cruise line."

"Did you leave Wolf at your place?"

"Yeah, he's off duty and not part of the team. Captain knows he's there but didn't want him read in, at least not yet."

"Copy that," Ryan said. It looked like they weren't getting any downtime between missions after all.

"I can't believe you really went running. I thought you were kidding last night," Rafe said.

"Why? It's not like I have a woman to keep me in bed all day."

Murph laughed. "Yeah it's not like we were doing squat thrusts in the cucumber patch."

"For fuck's sake, how the hell do you come up with that shit?" Ryan asked and chuckled at the look on Rafe's face.

"Hell, I don't know. I'm just talented I guess," Murph said.

"You wanna get your happy asses inside?" Jake said as he held open the briefing room door.

"Sorry, boss," Murph said as and he followed Jake into the room.

Cam and Halo were already at the table when the rest of the Black Eagle team followed Jake into the room. Captain Knox waited for them to get settled.

"Sorry to bring you all back in, but this came down this morning and..." There was a knock at the door, before it opened. Their heads swiveled as one toward the door. He shouldn't have been surprised to see Chrissy walk into the room.

"I apologize for being late, Captain."

"No worries. Take a seat." She looked around the room and sat next to Jake in the only open seat.

Fuck. If she was sitting, then she wasn't part of the briefing and that meant only one thing. She was part of the op. Why would they send an analyst instead of a seasoned field agent?

Rafe kicked Ryan under the table and pulled his attention back to the briefing.

"As I was saying, this came down the chain this morning. The Coasties reported a series of incidents with the Island Sun Cruise line. The FBI is also investigating, and the NSA got involved somehow. You wouldn't know anything about that would you?"

Ryan figured it was probably Tex helping move things along after what he'd dug up last night.

"No, sir," Jake answered after a moment's hesitation. He was sure Knox had his suspicions, but he left it alone.

"Wolf Steel and his wife had tickets for the next cruise but are going to transfer them to their 'friends' since he has to get back to work. It's an option the cruise line offered due to the delay. Ryan and Ms. Stillwell will go in their place. The rest of team will be split up, two in Puerto Rico and two with the Coasties."

"How are we going to get weapons on a cruise ship?" Murph asked.

"You're not. But the FBI is going to help us out there. They have an agent embedded with one of the delivery services stocking the food. He'll hide a small weapons package for you."

As soon as Ryan heard his name his gut twisted. The two of them stuck in a room on a cruise ship. Maybe he was still sleeping because it sure as hell felt like a nightmare.

"Why not send an experienced agent?" Ryan asked, knowing he was asking for trouble.

"I asked for her. She knows more about this op than anyone and she's worked us before."

The glance Jake gave Ryan said drop it. And he had no choice. Unless he could come up with an excellent reason not to, he'd be in close quarters with Chrissy for the duration of the cruise.

"I can handle myself. I joined the FBI to be a field agent." Why wasn't she then? It was none of his business, but it didn't mean he didn't want to know. If she had issues that could be a liability in the field he needed to be prepared.

"The ship is due back in port late this afternoon and going back out tomorrow. That gives us about a bit over twenty-four hours to prep."

"What is the plan for Puerto Rico?"

"You need to figure out what's actually going on when the ship docks. So many unscheduled stops is too much of a coincidence. Something is definitely going on."

"We'll be running point, but the FBI and Coasties will be on standby to assist."

"Any other questions?"

"What about backup if Ryan needs it?" Murph asked.

"Historically there haven't been any issues on the ship until the return leg," Chrissy said. "We shouldn't encounter any problems before then."

"We can't count on that. We'll need to be ready for anything," Ryan added. It probably pissed her off, but he wanted to make sure she realized the danger. If what she believed was true, these were men who would stop at nothing to accomplish their mission.

"Follow up briefing tomorrow at oh seven hundred." Knox left them to figure out the details. They were used to having a liaison, Bill Lynch had been with them for years until the clusterfuck in Saudi Arabia. But he'd been an experienced agent, Chrissy was green, stubborn, and he never knew what would set her off. He'd have to spend half his time keeping the little hellion out of trouble. If something happened to her he'd never forgive himself.

"Don't worry about me. I can take care of myself."

"How long has it been since you even held a gun?"

"I go to the range at least once a month. I won't be a liability."

Ryan and Rafe exchanged glances and Rafe shrugged. It was a mission, these were the parameters, it wasn't going to change, and they'd all deal with whatever came their way.

"Chrissy, what have you come up with so far?" Jake asked.

They sat at the table for the next two hours going over everything she already figured out. From the shady way the cruise company appeared out of nowhere two years earlier, to the all coincidental disasters on cruise after cruise. They could be up to almost anything.

By the time they were done, they had the details nailed down, with options B, C and D mapped out. Backup plans were essential and had saved their lives more times than he could count.

CHAPTER 5

A cruise. Most of her classmates at Quantico would have killed to have this for their first field assignment. Excitement sizzled through her body. She could barely keep from jumping up and down like a little kid as she got out her suitcase and sifted through her clothes. There were more discarded than kept. She'd have to go shopping. Good thing they didn't sail until tomorrow. Ugh, they. Ryan. Of all the SEALs on Black Eagle Team, why did they pick him for her partner?

Would he be a distraction? For sure. Mr. Pissy Pants drove her out of her mind. She spent her time around him being torn between the desire to jump his bones and rip his head off. But she'd be damned if she'd let it impact her first mission in the field.

The familiar ringtone from Friends filled her bedroom. Fuck. Meghan. She couldn't tell her anything about the mission, but she couldn't just disappear for a week either.

"Hi, Meggy. Are you enjoying your house guests?"

"They just left. No cruise for them. I could tell how disappointed Caroline was, but Matthew promised to see if they could find a short cruise on the west coast when they got home."

"That's great. I really liked them."

"Me too. If Rafe and I get out to California we have an open invite to stay with them."

"So when are you leaving?"

"Not anytime soon. Rafe's heading out tomorrow."

"Oh, really?"

"Yeah. Should I plan a girl's night for Friday? I'm sure Miranda would be all over it. She still gets a little freaked out when Cam leaves."

"I love girls' nights, but I won't be around. I took your advice."

"You did? I can't keep track of all the advice

I've given you that you haven't taken. What are you doing?"

"I'm going on a cruise."

"No fucking way."

"Geesh, I figured you'd be thrilled. I'll be getting away, out on the open water, nothing but blue skies and lots of drinking."

"I wasn't born yesterday. You're an analyst, not James Bond."

"Whoa, that was quite a jump…"

"I know, you can't tell me, but it's too much of a coincidence and neither of us believe in those. If you didn't want me to know, you should have been more careful last night."

It had been a shot in the dark that Meghan would buy her excuse, so she wasn't surprised it hadn't worked. "I'm not going to discuss this with you. The only thing I'm going to say is that I graduated at the top of my class at Quantico. I am more than qualified for anything I want or am assigned to do, and you know it."

Meghan's sigh was audible. It didn't matter if anyone else was happy about this, Chrissy was going. "Want to come shopping with me? I need to pick up a few things for my trip."

"Guns? Knives? Ammo?"

"Funny. I was thinking a bathing suit, shorts, shirts and something to wear for dinner in case there's something fancy."

"You're serious?"

"Yes, why wouldn't I be?"

"Fucking crazy, that's what you are. It's not that I don't have every confidence in your abilities, but this is freaking dangerous. And you and Rafe will be gone at the same time. He usually has more down time between missions." Wait for it. Meghan was about to have a volcanic eruption. Her bestie was smart and would put two and two together in three, two, one…

"Oh my God. You're going on a mission with Rafe, aren't you?"

"I can neither confirm nor deny."

"Fuck. This was never an option I'd considered. At least he'll keep an eye on you. But, this is so not cool."

"I don't know what you're talking about. But I really do need to go shopping. Are you coming or not?"

"Yeah, I'm coming."

"You'd better have your happy let's spend

money face on, or I'll dump you by the side of the road."

Chrissy smiled at her whispered 'bitch.' "Fine."

"I'll be there in about ten minutes."

Meghan still looked pissed when Chrissy picked her up fifteen minutes later. Before she left, she pulled up the website for the Island Sun Cruises to see the dress code. It was only the third time they'd been to the MacArthur Center, but it had all of their favorite shops and she had a list of things she needed. In the end, Meghan talked her into three fancy dresses she'd probably never wear, and a much sexier swimsuit than she wanted. What the hell, maybe it would keep Ryan distracted enough to stop hassling her.

If she hadn't known better, she'd have been sure that Meghan knew she was going undercover with Ryan. But there was no way. She couldn't read minds and Rafe hadn't even been home yet, not that he'd slip about the mission.

After three hours of shopping and spending way too much money, they stopped and had a late lunch at a little Mexican place in the mall they'd heard was good. Mexican was one of her favorites after pizza. They both ordered the Taqueria Sopes. The fried dough filled with seasoned chicken topped with onions and cilantro made her mouth water as soon as the waiter put it in front of her. Chrissy managed to eat it all even, after sharing a large guacamole with Meghan while they waited.

"Damn, I won't fit in my new clothes. There will be bulges in all the wrong places." Meghan laughed. "You know that's not possible. You've always been tall, thin and I've always been jealous."

"That makes two of us, I've been jealous of your curves since they showed up in junior high. I guess we always want what we don't have."

"Ain't that the truth. It's how the stores make so much money."

"Well, now that we managed to blow my clothing budget for the next two years, are you ready to go home?"

"Shit. Good thing my blog has been taking off, or I'd be dipping into my savings account to cover these bills. Who knew that shopping with you would cost me so much money."

"Broke friends love company." They giggled

as they gathered their bags. "Just promise me you won't do anything stupid. I know you think you have everything figured out, but we also know it's not always true."

Chrissy closed her eyes to try to block out the memory from four years ago. It had been her one big fuck up and almost cost her everything. The meltdown during training when she had convinced herself there was a real threat, almost got her kicked out of the academy. If it hadn't been for one of her instructors siding with her, she'd have been out on her ass. It had taken her a while to get her confidence back and to trust herself again.

'I will make sure to be protected at all times. We sure bought enough sunscreen. I can probably cover the entire ship in it." It was all she could say, but Meghan understood and nodded. Then she dropped her bags on the floor and pulled her into a tight hug. "Easy girl, I'm too full for that much squeezing."

"Yeah, no shit. I don't know what Rafe is going to do for dinner because I don't think I can eat for a week after that." As always, that's all it took for the tension to dissipate. True friends to the end, and Chrissy hoped that wouldn't be for a long, long time..

~

Frustrated, pissed off, so angry, he barely stopped himself from punching the wall. Why pair him with Chrissy? Wouldn't Rafe have been a better choice? They knew each other a lot better. Or even Murph. Basically, anyone but him.

"I chose you for two reasons. One, you have chemistry whether you want to admit it or not, it's visible to everyone around you. And two, because I know you'll do what it takes to keep her safe and still listen to her. Rafe would assume he knew the right thing to do. Murph wouldn't hear her, he'd just blow things up. But you will, and if it goes sideways you'll be able to keep her alive until help gets there," Jake said as if he'd voiced his thoughts out loud.

"I didn't ask…"

"No, but I can feel the tension coming off of you in waves. I know you all inside and out, it's my job to know how you'll react, or not react."

"Makes sense."

"Yes, it does. Do you understand why I chose you now?"

"Yes, but I'm still not happy about it."

"Fuck, Ryan, lately you haven't been happy about much. You might need to have a forced leave if you don't figure out what's up your ass. I can't have you putting the team or yourself in jeopardy because your head isn't in the game."

"I'm always focused when we're working. You know it too, or you'd have benched me."

Jake smiled. Ryan had no doubt that if he thought he wasn't on he'd never have chosen him to be coupled with Chrissy for this.

"You're right. But it doesn't mean I can't change my mind. Don't push me."

"Copy that, Boss. See you in the morning."

When he got outside, he was surprised to see Rafe leaning against the side of his truck. "What's up, bro?"

"I wanted to make sure you were okay. This mission on top of the last one sucks, but having to protect Chrissy..."

"I'm fine. Seriously. No worries. If the intel she's dug up is right, it'll be a boring week wandering around the ship trying to figure out if anything is going on. It'll be cushy, unlike yours."

"Ehh, wherever Murph and I hole up will be better than the shit show in Syria."

"Truth. I wonder what's going on with the chemist. Think he was telling the truth about working against his will?"

"No, I don't. Do you?"

"Fuck no. He's dirty. I just hope we caught him before he delivered whatever they'd requested."

"It's up to the CIA now. I'm sure they have him in some black sight picking his brain apart a little at a time."

"Good riddance, with any luck he'll rot there for the rest of his life."

"Amen to that."

"I have to figure out what to bring on the mission. I can't remember the last time I wore a suit. But I don't suppose I can get away with my dress blues."

"I don't think so," Rafe said with a wink. Ryan had one suit from his mother's funeral. It was three years old and hadn't been out of his closet once since that day. He doubted it even fit him anymore.

"I guess I'm going shopping."

"Good luck with that. Check the website and

see if there is a dress code. Maybe you'll get lucky. Call if you need to vent."

"Thanks. I'll be fine." Climbing into his truck, he tossed his duffel into the back seat. Next stop home for a shower, then he'd worry about packing.

After his shower, he pulled up the website for Island Sun Cruises. Relieved they had a casual dress code and jackets were optional, Ryan didn't have to shop at all. He pulled together a week's worth of acceptable cruise clothing in a real suitcase. That was the strange part. He was used to carrying packs for everything, but this time he'd have to blend in and look like every other cruise passenger. Tempted to try to pack at least one of his favorite knives, he decided against it in the end. If security was on point, he didn't need to be detained and blow the op.

Staring at the suit in his closet brought back all the memories of his mother's funeral. It had been a beautiful sunny day and all their friends had attended and then went back to the house afterward. He'd been a late in life baby after they'd given up trying to have a second child. Patrick, his older brother, was almost twelve by the time Ryan had come along.

Their family was just him and his dad now. Losing his brother in Afghanistan was the reason he'd joined the Navy to become a SEAL. It was also the reason he chose to avoid relationships. Relationships were difficult and messy, but also wonderful if you used his parent's for an example.

It had been a couple of months since he'd called his dad. He needed to do better, especially since he was almost seventy and living alone. There wasn't much left in the house since he hadn't shopped yet, but there was always peanut butter and jelly. Whipping up a quick sandwich, he carried it into the living room and stretched out on the couch with the plate balanced on his stomach. Pulling his phone from his pocket, he called his dad.

It rang three times before Brian McLaughlin picked up the phone.

"Hello?" No cell phone or caller ID for his dad. The man believed in landlines only.

"Hi, Dad. It's Ryan."

"Hey, Son. How are you? Is everything okay?"

"Yeah, everything's fine. How are you doing?"

"Good, good. I was out watering your mother's garden. It's still blooming. I swear that woman had the greenest thumb on the planet and it's still working even without her here. Or maybe she's watching over it."

"Maybe." Ryan smiled. His dad was right, his mother's garden was always featured in the neighborhood newsletter. She could make anything grow. "You feeling okay? Staying busy?"

"Yeah, I'm fine. In fact, I had a checkup last week and the doc said I was in great shape."

"Glad to hear that. I wish you were closer so I could keep an eye on you."

"I am perfectly capable of taking care of myself. You have an important job. You don't need to be worrying about me."

"If you say so."

"I do. Now tell me what's the real reason you called? You gonna get married, give me a grandchild?"

Ryan laughed. "I swore I could hear Mom's voice right then. Sorry, Dad, I'm not getting married. I'm not even dating."

"Why not? You're thirty-three years old. What are you waiting for?"

"I don't have time for a woman."

"That's bullshit, young man. You can't let

what happened with Patrick and Darlene keep you from finding happiness."

"I'm not."

"Really? Then what's stopping you?"

"Damn, you're worse than mom. I just don't think it's fair to bring a woman into my life. Not with how I live."

"You have friends who have relationships, right?"

"Yes, but as you used to tell me when I was little, if Bobby jumped off the bridge would you do it too?"

"What if I told you that being with the right woman is the most fulfilling relationship you'll ever have. That they fill in all the missing gaps in your life and you feel whole."

"I'd say that's great for some, but not for me."

"So, there's someone you like?"

"I didn't say that."

"You didn't have to. I could hear it in your voice. What's her name?"

"I'm not doing this with you, Dad. Let's talk about what you're doing? I hope you're not holing up in the house all by yourself all the time."

"I joined a widower's group. We go golfing

and have movie nights. I probably get out more than you. In fact, we're going to the movies tonight."

"That's great to hear."

"When are you coming to visit? Christmas at least?"

"I'll try. I promise."

"Sounds good. Or maybe I'll have to come visit you. You have a spare bed at your place?"

"I do."

"Good. Okay, I'm going to let you go. I'm sure you have stuff to do. I'll talk to you soon, Son. And give that woman a call and see what happens."

Ryan rolled his eyes. What was it with people as they got older? Always pushing everyone to get married, have kids, set down roots. Now he remembered why it had been so long since he'd called him.

Finishing his sandwich, he put the plate on the coffee table and grabbed the remote. Anything to get the conversation out of his head. Every time he even thought about giving in to his attraction to Chrissy, he could see Darlene's face as she found out her husband was never coming home again. After that everything had gone to shit. She'd been eight months pregnant and went into labor from the shock. They lost the baby and then she gave up on life. A few months later they found her dead in her room, with an empty bottle of pills by her side. It was horrible. Women shouldn't have to wait, praying they don't see that car show up in front of their home.

CHAPTER 6

Chrissy tossed and turned for most of the night until she gave up trying to sleep. There was too much going through her mind to let her rest. It was like trying to sleep the night before the first day of school. She always woke up on and off all night worried she'd be late. It happened every year and even when she was at the FBI Academy in Quantico.

The rain was pouring down like buckets, but it did nothing to dull the excitement and trepidation of her first field assignment. Sometime between two and three a.m. she realized there was a hint of fear in the midst of the anticipation. What if she let the guys down? What if she was wrong? And worst of all, what if she got one of them killed?

Doubt was her worst enemy and she couldn't let it win. She had the intel, and if the SEALs were involved it wasn't just her intel that prompted the mission. This is what she did, where she excelled. Now she had a chance to prove it to everyone, but most of all, to herself.

While she waited for the coffee to brew, she went through the clothing she'd purchased with Meghan. Selecting a pair of blue capris and a blue and white-striped shirt, she dressed quickly and slipped on a pair of navy blue flats. It was like playing dress up with Meghan when they were young. But this time there were lives involved.

Double checking to make sure she had everything she needed, she zipped up the suitcase and rolled it into the living room and grabbed a cup of coffee. It was only five a.m. and she didn't have to be at Little Creek until seven. As she sipped the hot liquid, her stomach twisted in knots and she wondered if the coffee had been a good idea.

How did the guys deal with this every time? Or maybe that was the trick. They'd been doing this forever, knowing they were leaving probably didn't faze them at all. Instead, she was sitting on the edge of the couch, her knees bouncing up and down when she had a sudden urge to toss her cookies. Fuck. Deep breaths, Chrissy. In. Out. In. Out. It was a cruise ship not the middle of Iraq.

Calm again, she flipped on the television. Not because she really cared, but to break the silence. When she'd had an almost breakdown at Quantico, the FBI doctor taught her breathing exercises and a few other tricks when she started to feel overwhelmed. She said that people with her 'skills' tended to get inundated by their surroundings when under extreme pressure. It was just too much to process at one time.

The method worked and she was able to stay and finish her training. Her parents and Meghan had come to her graduation and for the first time in her life, Chrissy felt like she belonged. Now she was taking her next step, one she'd expected to take years ago. Her analyst skills had been more important then, and probably were now. If it hadn't been for Captain Knox, she'd still be at her desk working on intel while another agent helped uncover whatever was going on with Island Sun cruises.

Ugh. Ryan. She'd managed to avoid thinking about him, but now he was dead center in her mind. What would it be like posing as a wife—his wife? He didn't look too thrilled yesterday when he found out. She made sure to get out of there before he could talk to her. The last thing she needed was an argument. Although, it was probably going to happen constantly while they were on the ship, if their prior meetings were any indication. The only time they'd managed to be civil was when they'd called a temporary truce the other night. Maybe that would be the trick, a truce while they were on the mission. Surely they could pull that off.

Finally it was time to go. With one last check of the apartment, then she grabbed her suitcase and headed out to her Jeep. She'd bet they'd be taking Ryan's truck to the port, but since no one had told her otherwise, she figured it was okay to leave the Jeep parked at Little Creek while they were gone.

It was still pouring rain, but traffic was light since it was only six fifteen. Little Creek was only about fifteen minutes from her home, so she'd make it in plenty of time and not be late like yesterday. It wasn't an impression she wanted to give the captain or any of the team.

The rain finally let up a bit as she pulled into the parking lot. She'd thought she was early, but she recognized several of their trucks. It was weird they all drove trucks. She should have asked Wolf if he drove one too. Maybe it was a SEAL thing. Grabbing her purse and umbrella, she left the suitcase in the Jeep and ran for the front door. Shaking off the excess water, she went up to the desk to sign in and get her visitor badge.

Her footsteps echoed as she walked down the hallway toward the briefing room. For the first time in her life, she understood the expression that the quiet was deafening. With each step the tension stiffened her shoulders and her stomach twisted tighter. Counting to ten under her breath, some of it eased as she approached the door. As she reached for the doorknob, it opened, and she stepped back far enough that the door didn't smack her in the head.

"Shit, Chrissy, I'm sorry. I didn't think anyone would be out here," Cam said with a smile. "I didn't hit you, did I?" Halo was at his side like always, tongue hanging out and waiting for Cam's next move.

"No, you missed."

"I'd have caught some serious shit if I knocked you out."

"Probably not, but no worries."

"I getting some coffee, want a cup?"

"That would be great. Thank you. Two sugars, light on the cream or milk, whatever you've got."

"Okay, be right back. Go on in."

He held the door while she went into the room and came face-to-face with Ryan. Great. At least he hadn't been the one to almost take her out with the door. She'd never have believed it was an accident.

"Morning, Chrissy. How are you?"

"I'm great. How about you?" Surprisingly, he grinned, and she felt like a deer in the headlights. What was up with that?

"Excellent. Ready to get married?"

"What?" She had to have heard him wrong. Either that or the man had lost his mind.

"The mission – husband and wife, remember?"

"Yeah, but we're not really getting married.

It's just our cover."

"I know, but the look on your face was priceless."

"Great. Thanks, trying to give me a heart attack will not make me quit the mission."

"Ehh, it was a worth a shot." This was the Ryan she was used to, all the snarky remarks. It's why she came up with his nickname. "I'm kidding. Seriously."

"Right. Prove it. Let's have a truce for the duration of the mission. We need to be able to work together and not be at each other's throats."

"I was going to propose the same thing, pun intended," Ryan said with a grin. She figured he was trying to ease the tension, but it just spun her up more. "But yeah, truce it is."

They were just sitting down when the door opened, and Cam came in holding a tray of coffees with Halo by his side, followed by Captain Knox. He distributed the coffees and took a seat at the table and waited for Knox to begin.

Glancing at Chrissy during the briefing, he had

to admit that she looked great and smelled amazing. He'd been surprised she suggested the truce, but at least they were on the same page. He'd decided last night that he would do all he could to keep her safe while letting her work her intel magic. If it hadn't been for her, they wouldn't have any idea about the cruise line at all.

Was he concerned about her getting into trouble? Hell yeah. She was a little hellion who didn't think before diving head first into whatever intrigued her. With the truce in place, maybe she'd be more open to listening to him.

There weren't any major updates since yesterday's briefing and their assignments were confirmed. The only additional information came from the Coast Guard. Murph and Rafe would be heading out first with the Coasties. Cam, Halo, and Jake's transport to Puerto Rico departed at eleven hundred.

After the briefing ended, Jake handed them the mission packet which included their wedding bands, identities–Ryan and Chrissy Bennett, and their boarding documents. Ryan laughed it off as he took the ring but sliding the thin gold band onto his finger sent a chill down his spine.

Chrissy didn't seem any happier about the

ring and he thought she might refuse to wear it. The color drained out of her cheeks when she dumped it into her hand but after a short hesitation she slipped it on.

It wasn't the only sign she wasn't entirely ready for the mission. Her knee bounced up and down under the table since she sat down. But it was the only outward sign of her state of mind. He'd have been worried if she wasn't stressed. Field work was dangerous, and it didn't matter how qualified anyone was, when it came down to it, reaction was key. If you couldn't think on your feet you were in deep shit. For Chrissy, thinking on her feet was as much as part of her as breathing. He hoped that it didn't desert her when she needed it most.

"Want to take a drive to kill some time?"

"Sure. That would be wonderful. Sitting here with nothing to do would drive me out of my mind."

"Same here. Do you want to drive?" The question seemed to surprise her.

"You'd let me drive you around?"

"Yeah, why not?"

"I don't know. I guess most of the men I know usually insist on driving."

"I'm not most men."

"You can say that again."

"Hey, what about the truce."

"Right, sorry. But you can drive. I wouldn't know where to go."

"Sure." He held the door for her and got another raised eyebrow. Seriously, what kind of men did she hang around with. His mom raised him to be a gentleman. But thinking about their interactions, he hadn't shown her that side of himself. He'd had his reasons, but for now, he needed to practice being a loving husband.

The rain stopped while they were in the briefing and the sky was clearing. It was a good omen for the cruise. It would be miserable if it rained, all the passengers would be stuck inside, and that would suck trying to get around the ship.

Ryan pulled out of the parking lot and headed toward the beach. The water soothed him, and he hoped it would have the same effect on Chrissy. Neither of them spoke, but the silence wasn't uncomfortable.

"I'm glad we don't have to be Wolf and Caroline. Knowing the real couple would be weird."

"I agree. It'll be much easier being able to use

our real first names. Less chance of a screw up."

Chrissy laughed, but he could hear her nervousness. "Yeah, you mean me screwing it up, right?"

"No, I meant either of us. I don't do a lot of this type of mission. We usually go in, get our guy and get out. But this is different. I'm hoping we can blend in and spend most of our time not interacting with anyone."

"That sounds perfect to me. I'm not very good in social situations when I don't know the people I have to be around."

"Really? I didn't get that impression when I first met you at Rafe's."

"Thanks, for saying that."

"I meant it. Maybe because you were with Meghan?"

"Maybe. Speaking of Meghan, I think she knows what we're doing. It's not like I just drop everything and go on vacation."

"Rafe said she was upset last night. Worried about you. Although he didn't confirm anything."

"Neither did I, but she's not stupid. Maybe if the whole Wolf and Caroline thing hadn't happened."

"Rafe wasn't worried, so you shouldn't be

either. Shit just happens."

"That's for sure. Oh, you drove us to the beach." Her smile lit up her whole face.

"Yeah. It's where I hang out whenever possible. It's my happy place."

"I'm kind of surprised since you have to spend so much time in the water."

"Didn't you know? I'm half fish."

"No," she replied with a laugh, throwing open the door as soon as he'd parked. Her excitement was contagious, and his mood lightened. By the time he got out of the truck she was almost at the water, her capris folded up and her shoes dangling from her fingers.

The wind blew her blonde hair around her face, her cheeks were a soft shade of pink, and her eyes danced with joy. The sight took his breath away. He didn't know if he was finally seeing the real Chrissy, or if the setting brought out something in her she'd kept hidden. He'd been attracted to her from the first time he'd met her, and that was why he gave her such a hard time and tried to keep her at a distance. The wall around his heart cracked a bit and feelings he'd vowed to ignore seeped in. If this was how the week with her was going to be, he was fucked.

Once he caught up to her, they walked along the water's edge. It was as close to a date as he'd been on since high school. Sure, he'd been with his share of women, but they knew it was just sex. It had been fine, until now. He had to fight the desire to reach out and take her hand. To pull her into his arms and find out if she tasted as good as she smelled. Yeah, he was definitely in deep shit.

"I'm glad you brought us here. I'd forgotten how much I love the beach."

"How long since you've been here?"

"Umm, probably about three years, maybe four. When I first moved here I'd try to come on the weekends, but then I threw myself into work. I didn't know anyone, and I don't make friends easily. Meghan was still in Atlanta..."

Her voice trailed off and he could almost feel how hard it had been for her to move far from everyone and everything she'd known. Jake let him read her file and he knew what she tried so desperately to hide. The eidetic memory, the issues growing up, the breakdown at Quantico. He'd been surprised he'd been read in, but Jake felt it was important to know as much as possible to make sure she stayed safe. It made him want to wrap her in his arms and go far away from the danger they were about to encounter.

Ryan debated telling her that he knew her secrets, but he didn't want to spoil her obvious enjoyment. And it would have, without a doubt. She'd have been furious to know her privacy was breached. She'd probably be shocked at how many people knew her abilities.

"You should try to come more often; the sea air is refreshing and good for you."

"Much better than cube living, that's for sure. And now we get a whole week of sea air."

"Yeah, but it isn't a vacation."

"I know. You really need to have more faith in me."

"I have faith. I just know how easily things can go FUBAR."

"I do know a little, Meghan told me what it was like when y'all rescued her and Miranda and the rest of the missionary workers. What you do is dangerous, and life threatening every time you go out. But I'm hoping this one will be different. We're looking for information, not taking down terrorists."

"Don't be so sure. You said they were escalating. We have to be ready for anything."

"I already planned for that. Since the cruise is shorter, they earliest they can pick up anyone would be the second day when we stop at Nassau."

"Right, I read that in the packet, but just because it will seem safe doesn't mean something isn't going on. There has to be someone on the ship that knows or is handling all of this. And so far we have no idea who that is."

"I know, that's my missing piece. I couldn't find anyone who was on the ship for each incident. It's making me crazy. The puzzle doesn't fit together without that piece."

"Have you considered that they are on the ship but aren't registered anywhere?"

"I considered it, but wouldn't that be hard to get passed customs and TSA going out?"

"It depends, or they could be using fake IDs. That's my guess. It would be the easiest way."

"I'd thought about that and then discarded it as low probability."

"Why?"

"It would involve too many extra people. More chance of discovery. Unless they are talented enough to make their own IDs."

"Fake IDs aren't hard to get."

"Maybe not, but they'd need a lot of them to have handled all of the incidents on the ships."

"Okay. I'll give you that. So we're back at square one."

"Exactly." They laughed.

"I guess we'll have to see what we can come up with. But for now, I think we need to head back to Little Creek so we can grab your bag and head to the port. Boarding starts in an hour."

"Wow. Already?"

"Yeah."

Chrissy turned and grabbed his hand. "Thank you for this. It was exactly what I needed." Her touch sent shockwaves up his arm. Surprise, and something more. Fuck. It was going to be a long 'hard' week in more ways than one.

"I'm glad you enjoyed it. Maybe we can do it again sometime."

"Yeah, I'd like that," Chrissy said with a big smile.

Holy fuck. He sounded like a lovesick kid. He needed to get his shit straightened out and fast. Now was not the time for everything he'd believed to get tossed into the ocean.

CHAPTER 7

The visit to the beach went a long way to soothing Chrissy's frayed nerves. It also helped her figure out it wasn't the mission freaking her out, but letting down the SEALs, especially Ryan. She might deny her attraction to everyone else, but the more time she spent with him the more intense it became. This week was going to be hell on her libido, even if he ended up being a total jackass. And after the last couple of hours, she had her doubts about that as well.

They'd stopped by Little Creek and she grabbed her suitcase from the Jeep. Their next stop—Port Norfolk. The Jewel made port the night before and had been cleaned and prepped for today's departure. It was four days behind schedule and there had been a lot of cancellations.

"Remember, we're married, happily married, right?" Ryan said as he pulled into the parking lot at the Cruise Terminal. "That means PDAs. Are you okay with that? I suppose I should have brought it up earlier."

"PDAs – oh, I got it. Yeah, I'm a grown woman, I can handle a few kisses. But I can't promise not to knee you in the family jewels if you go too far. Instinct, you know," she said with a forced grin. Fuck. She hadn't considered the ramifications of posing as a married couple. Her concentration had been focused solely on the mission, or rather the terrorist portion. At least she'd earn a new nickname. Horniest woman at sea. It was much better than freak, psycho, and all of the others she'd accrued in high school.

"Good. I'll try to keep my wandering hands to a minimum." Ryan grinned and took her suitcase from her hand.

"What are you doing?"

"What?"

"I can handle my own suitcase."

"Of course you can, but what kind of a considerate husband would I be if I let you?"

Chrissy rolled her eyes. She wasn't sure if he was teasing, or if this was the real Mr. Pissy Pants. If so, she'd judged him way wrong. For some reason, her reasoning abilities went south whenever she got close to him.

"Fine." Then she mumbled, "This is going to be a long cruise." Apparently he possessed supersonic hearing since his laugh was loud enough for everyone near them to turn and look. "I get it now, you're going to be so nice, I'm going to need a dentist to fill my cavities by the time we get back."

"No, way. I'm just trying to play my part."

"I see."

"You need to lighten up a little. Your expression is so intense you're scaring people."

"It's not."

"It is. A smile would go a long way to convincing people I wasn't dragging you on the ship against your will."

Chrissy sighed. He was right. What was wrong with her? It's like all of her circuits were crossed at the worst possible time. Mentally kicking herself in the ass, she plastered a big smile on her face and punched Ryan in the side, in a loving kind of way.

"Oomph, was that a love tap?"

Smiling up at him, with what she hoped was an evil glint in her eye, she answered, "Yup, and there's a lot more where that came from, Pooky."

"Pooky?"

"Yes. Would you rather I call you something else?" It was his turn to sigh. This time she laughed. If she could keep her hormones in check this might be kind of fun, especially since it looked like he could dish it out better than he could take it. Truce or not there were ways around everything.

The Jewel could only support up to four hundred and fifty passengers and was considered a midsized ship, as were all the Island Sun Cruise line's ships. Smaller meant less decks to cover while they searched the ship, it also meant it would be harder to avoid notice by the crew members.

Overwhelmed by the sea of people, Chrissy stopped when they entered the crowded terminal. It was too loud and too chaotic. Ryan's hand at the base of her spine reminded her she wasn't alone. Taking a deep breath she stepped into the crowd and made her way toward security.

While waiting in line, she pulled out their

boarding documents and passports from her purse. Security wasn't as strict as at the airport, and she was able to keep her shoes on and didn't even have to take her tablet out of her purse. Their luggage was scanned since they'd only brought carry-on bags, and then they went through the x-ray machines.

"So far so good," she whispered to Ryan as they moved to the next part of the process. The cruise employees lined them up in sections for check-in. From the length of the lines, she figured they'd be there for an hour at least, but it moved quickly. Soon it was their turn.

"Welcome to Island Sun Cruises. May I have your name and travel documents?"

"Hi. We're the Barretts."

"Welcome, Mr. and Mrs. Barrett. We're excited to have you sail with us. Can you fill out this form to verify you haven't been ill recently."

They filled out the forms and handed them back to the smiley cruise employee. Chrissy wondered if her cheeks hurt at the end of the day from smiling.

"Great, we're almost done. I need a photo for security purposes. Please look this way," Ms. Happy Pants said and pointed at the camera mounted on her computer monitor. "Thank you. These are your Cruise Cards. They will get you into your room and are used for everything on the cruise. Try not to lose them."

"Thank you," Ryan said as he took the cards from her.

"Also, here is the schedule for today and a map of the Jewel. Enjoy your cruise."

"Thank you again," Chrissy said and took the map and shoved it into her purse to examine later. She wasn't as interested in the schedule, but it might come in handy.

Neither of them had been on a cruise before and had been surprised at all the steps they'd had to go through before they were finally able to embark. Following signs for the Jewel they passed through the terminal door and were greeted by a group of photographers.

"May we take a souvenir photo? You can pick it up on the third day of the cruise if you like it, but there's no obligation to purchase it."

Chrissy and Ryan exchanged glances, her first instinct was to say no and move on, but it wouldn't suit their cover. Almost as if Ryan read her mind, he nodded. "Sure, we'd love it, right,

Pooky?" His cringe at her pet name made her smile even wider.

"Stand right here and smile." It took all of ten seconds for the entire process, it was like a production line in a factory they way they move them right along from station to station. Next they were cleared for boarding and finally made their way up the gangway. Chrissy had been wondering if they'd ever get on the damn ship.

"Are we having fun yet," Ryan whispered as they reached the end of the gangway and stepped onto the ship.

"I haven't decided. I wasn't expecting all of this just to get on board." Before she could say anything else a member of the crew stepped up to greet them.

"Welcome aboard the Jewel. May I see your cruise card?" Chrissy handed her card to a tall, dark, and gorgeous man in uniform. If the rest of the crew was like him, it was going to be like her own Fantasy Island episode.

"You'll be staying on deck five and cabin number five oh eight. You can take the elevator to your left, or you're welcome to visit any of our restaurants or tour the ship."

"Thank you," Chrissy answered as he

returned her card. “Pooky, do you want to eat or go to the room first?” Damn, she loved calling him that and watching his reaction. By the end of the cruise, he’d never want to hear that word, if it really was a word, again.

“I think room first then food, darling. If that’s okay?” Darling? Ehh, it could have been so much worse. If they had to keep this up for long, they were both going to need a dentist at the end of the cruise.

“Yes, I can’t wait to see our suite,” she answered as they walked to the elevators. “Did you check them out online?”

“Yeah, I did. I wanted to find out the dress code, so I’d know what to pack.”

Chrissy grinned. “Me too. I have to keep telling myself this isn’t a vacation.”

“Exactly. It’ll be easy to get swept up into all of whatever this is, but we have a job to do.”

“I know, but we also have to fit in, so that means having a little fun while we check out the ship.”

Another couple joined them as they waited for the elevator before he could answer, but she caught his eye roll. As sexy as the crew dude was, he had nothing on Ryan. The first time she’d met him at Rafe and Meghan's, she had to make sure her mouth wasn't hanging open. Broad shouldered, that beautiful auburn hair, and his emerald green eyes fueled her fantasies for months. It was like he'd walked off the pages of Men's Health Magazine. And no, she didn't subscribe, but she couldn't resist flipping through it in the dentist's office. Just because she didn't date, didn't mean she was oblivious.

Wowzah. And she should have known better than to tell Meghan to. Then she wouldn't have to keep telling her that she wasn't interested. But nope, she'd made the mistake of telling her that he was hot. Hot damn. But it didn't matter he was off limits, and so far out of her league she wasn't even in the same zip code. And even if she'd wanted to pursue it, once he found out about her weirdness, he'd take off so fast her head would spin.

"You okay?" Ryan asked and squeezed her shoulder.

"Yeah, why?"

"You haven't heard a word I've said, have you?"

Shit. He'd been talking to her and she was off in her own world. "Sorry, Pooky, I was thinking about what we should do next. This schedule has lots of stuff to do today." He wasn't buying it, but he didn't call her on it. There were just too many people around.

Ryan didn't know if she was doing her puzzle solving or if something else was going on. But she had definitely zoned out. He wondered if she'd tell him about her skills while they were stuck on this ship, though it wasn't likely considering their adversarial relationship. He'd love to ask her questions about how she puts the pieces together, but the last thing he needed was his little hellion to flip out and blow their cover.

She was a loose cannon, an unknown, skills or not, and he couldn't take any chances. He had no idea how she'd react under pressure and he hoped he wouldn't have to find out.

"Hey, this is it, cabin five oh eight." He'd been concentrating on checking for cameras and thinking about her, that he he'd almost walked right past their cabin.

"Gotta love small ships. Some of the others are more like floating cities."

He stood by while she used the cruise card to open the door and pushed it open. "Holy fuck."

He followed her into the suite. It was the best part of this cruise line. All the cabins were suites. If they'd been in one of those little closets most ships called a standard room, he'd have lost his mind.

"I knew we had a suite, but this is so much more than I'd expected. And the view. Wow."

"The extra space is definitely a bonus," he said as he followed her into the room and closed the door. "I'll take the couch and you can have the bed." He'd hoped they'd have one of the rooms with the two doubles, but this was one queen, and that would put him too close to temptation.

"Maybe we can alternate. It's not fair that you sleep on the couch."

"It's not a big deal. As far as missions go, sleeping on a couch for a week is a luxury accommodation."

Chrissy grinned. "If you say so. But I bet after the second night you'd wish you took me up on my offer."

"We'll see. I brought coms so we can talk to each other if we have to split up and talk to Murph and Rafe when they get here."

“Perfect. I brought a few cool things too. Including these,” she said while reaching into her purse and pulling out an eyeglass case. “They’re not real glasses, the lens is clear, and I can take pictures by touching the side of the frame.”

“Spy toys, huh?”

“Not as fun as James Bond’s toys, but still pretty cool, no?”

“Yeah, cool, and handy for when shooting photos with our phones would be conspicuous.”

“Exactly, and they automatically upload to my laptop. I brought a SAT phone to use as our own hotspot, so we don’t have to use the ship’s public Wi-Fi.”

“Did you bring anything else?”

“No, Pierson said it was too risky since they could search our room anytime they want.”

“Good. I was hoping we wouldn’t have to figure out where to hide any other equipment. A laptop and glasses can sit in plain sight and no one would think twice about it.”

“You don’t have to worry about me. I’ve told you, I’m fully capable, I have a brown belt in Krav Maga. Even without a gun, I’m not helpless.”

“Fair enough.” He wanted to tell her that no

matter how experienced she was in a classroom setting. It wasn't close to reality, but it wouldn't matter. Part of his mission was to ensure she'd never need to defend herself. "I think we should get something to eat and then go exploring. Hit every deck we can. Then tonight, after we set sail, we'll see if we can get to the crew deck."

"Sounds like a plan." Ryan grabbed his bag and unpacked. It was weird for him since missions meant living out of his pack, but they needed to look like every other passenger on the ship.

"Did you see some of these people with their three and four suitcases and carry-ons too?"

"Yeah, they're crazy. Why would you need so much shit? You wouldn't believe what I usually have in my pack."

"Oh, I bet I would. Meghan's told me what comes out of Rafe's."

"I was glad you didn't have a bunch of luggage. Some women can't resist packing their entire closets."

"And you know this how? From experience?"

"Not experience, just an observation. I'm very observant."

"Oh really? I'll have to test you on that one."

With her usual short fuse, he worried that she'd taken his comment the wrong way. But seeing her shoulders shake and hearing the laughter she was trying to muffle, made him grin. His hellion was at it again.

CHAPTER 8

"Where to first?" Chrissy asked after they'd finished unpacking. Spreading the ship's map on the table, she went over all the decks one by one. "There's not a lot going on right now. I bet most people are wandering around. We could blend in and not look nosey."

"I agree, but first I need to get something to eat. I'm starving." It had been hours since her morning coffee and she hadn't eaten anything. Food was definitely a good idea.

"The main restaurant is here but I think that won't be open until dinner," she said and pointed it out on the map. "Here and here are casual places, this one is a like an Italian Bistro, and this is a hamburger joint."

"Stop, you had me at hamburger."

"Okay, you got it. Burger Joint it is."

"It that what it's called?"

"Yup, see, right here."

"Did you memorize the whole map?"

Shit. Of course he'd notice. It was part of the SEAL training. If she didn't want him to figure her out, she'd have to be more careful. "Just where the restaurants are. I must be hungry too."

"That makes sense. Good thing it's not one of those mega ships. You'd have lost your mind trying to find all of the restaurants on one of those."

"Probably. I better bring it with us. We don't need to get lost while exploring," Chrissy said as she folded the map and tucked it into her purse. "Ready?"

"Hell yeah. Can't you hear my stomach growling?"

"That's the noise I just heard? I figured it was the ship."

"Nope, just a hungry frogman," Ryan said with a grin. "C'mon, woman, before I eat my arm." Who was this Ryan and where had he come from? If he kept this up, she'd need to reconsider his nickname after the mission.

There hadn't been any sign of Mr. Pissy Pants all day.

The Burger Joint was up one deck and they decided to take the stairs. Chrissy had her glasses on and snapped photos to review later. She didn't need them, but Ryan would, and she wasn't ready to share her puzzle powers with him yet, or maybe ever. An eidetic memory was virtually unheard of in adults. After people found out, they tended to avoid her. She was happy they hadn't tried to use her as a guinea pig.

Ryan held the door open for her, and she walked into the eatery and back in time to the fifties. It looked just like what she'd imagine a soda shop would have been back then—metal stools at the counter and red leather booths with Formica tabletops.

"This is cool," Chrissy said as the hostess told them to grab a seat anywhere.

"I haven't seen a place like this in years. There was an old diner near my parent's house that looked a lot like this."

"Where was that?"

"A small town in Vermont." She wanted to ask him more, but it would have to wait until they ordered.

"Hi, I'm Maryann, welcome to the Burger Joint. Would you like to hear about today's specials?"

"Sure," Ryan said without hesitation.

"It's meatloaf, mashed potatoes, gravy and green beans, with fresh apple pie for dessert. You can have your choice of a non-alcoholic drink and it's only fifteen ninety-five."

"Thank you."

"Here's your menus. Can I get you something to drink?"

"Water for me," Chrissy answered. She'd have loved a chocolate milk shake, but the carbs would probably have knocked her out.

"I'll have a water and the largest root beer float you can make."

"You got it. I'll be right back with your drinks."

"I didn't see that coming."

"What? The float? Why?"

"I don't know. Just didn't seem to fit with what I know about you."

"Well, you don't know much then. I love root beer floats, and I even make them at home."

"No wonder you run ten miles every day."

"Hey. Are you implying I'm a little pudgy?"

"Not at all," she said with a giggle. Then she stuck her head in the menu before Maryann got back. They had work to do. It would be too easy to forget that they weren't on vacation.

"Have you decided?" Maryann said as she put their drinks on the table. The root beer float looked damn good, and she was a little envious.

"I'll have a bacon cheeseburger. Can I substitute onion rings for the French fries?"

"No problem. How do you want your burger cooked?"

"Medium is fine."

"And you, Sir?"

"I'll have what she's having except make it a double cheeseburger."

"Okay great. Let me know if you need anything."

"It's hard to believe we're actually on a cruise ship," Chrissy said as the waitress walked away to put in their order. The restaurant was fairly crowded, but surprisingly quiet.

"It is. I think the guys are going to be jealous."

"Probably. At least, until the shit hits the fan."

"I'm hoping to avoid any flying shit. But we'll see. Speaking of that, can I take a look at the map?"

"Sure." She pulled it out of her purse and handed it to him. He spread it out.

"We're on deck six, our cabin is on five, so we have a lot of exploring to do."

"Where should we start?"

"We might as well explore this one after we eat, and then go from there. The casino and the club room is on this level."

"What's the club room?"

"It sounds like dancing and a bar."

"Okay. We can skip that."

"Don't you dance?"

"Hell no. Only if you want a broken leg or worse. No dancing for me." The last time Chrissy had tried to dance it had been at a high school dance. She'd somehow managed to trip Meghan, who went flying across the floor in her heels, twisted her ankle, and took out three other people. Yeah, no she didn't need a repeat of that. It even made the yearbook.

"I think we'll have to check it out, but we don't have to dance." How did she know he'd say that?

"Fine."

Maryann was back with their orders. She

pulled the map off the table so it wouldn't get covered in burger grease.

"Holy crap, this is huge. How are you going to eat a double?" Chrissy asked as she looked at what had to be at least a half-pound burger and huge pile of onion rings.

"Watch me. I could probably finish whatever you don't."

As the food on his plate methodically disappeared, she believed him. Chrissy got through about half of her burger and some of the rings, but Ryan didn't finish her plate. Everything was delicious. No wonder people complained about gaining weight on cruises.

Ryan signed for the meal and left a tip on the table. "Ready to go?"

Nodding, she grabbed her purse and followed him out. "Which way?"

"You pick. We need to cover every inch of the ship. It doesn't matter where we start."

"Let's go right."

"We're looking for anything that doesn't seem quite right. Or if someone seems out of place."

"Yup, got it. I was at the briefing too."

"Sorry. It's habit. I'm used to going over

everything down to the slightest detail over and over, before we execute the mission."

"I get it. In a way I do the same thing, except it's all on paper or images."

"Yeah, that makes sense. You'd want to double, and triple check your facts. Based on your information nothing should happen on this cruise, right?"

"Maybe. The pattern was every other cruise, but then the last two had issues. Makes me think they're building up to something."

"I really hope you're wrong."

"Me too. So far they've been careful and only the ship has been damaged, none of the passengers or crew. Which is one of the reasons it jumped out at me."

"Because no one was hurt?"

"Yeah. How many times can there be a fire, or a problem with the engine, and no one gets hurt?"

"It's impressive that you discovered this."

"Thanks, but it's my job, and until now it was all behind a desk. I'd be lying if I didn't admit I'm stoked to have this chance."

"Jake said you wanted to be a field agent?"

"Yeah, but they decided they needed my

analytical skills more. It sucked in the beginning. I wanted to help make a difference. Eventually, I realized I was, just not the way I'd intended."

"You have your chance now. Let's just make sure you don't get hurt in the process."

"What about you, Pooky? You could get hurt."

"Again with the Pooky. You're killing me. Isn't there something else you could come up with?" Smooth subject change. She wondered how often he'd done that over the years.

"Nope. I like Pooky. It fits you," Chrissy answered and winked. She was doing it to get under his skin, but it wasn't working in the way she'd hoped. What he wanted to do was push her against a wall and kiss her until she begged him to stop. But it would be a huge mistake. "Besides, I heard you call me hellion when you talk to the guys."

"What? How…I'm going to kill Rafe one of these days."

"It's your fault, you should have known he'd mention it to Meghan or she'd over hear you say it."

"Yup. But I didn't mean it in a bad way."

"Sure. Do you know the definition of hellion? Not exactly the most flattering thing I've been called. But come to think of it, it's not the worst either."

"I'm sorry. I only meant that you are bull headed and when you get an idea you won't let go." It wasn't the full truth, she drove him out of his mind, digging, digging, digging at him usually. But something changed the last time they'd been at Meghan and Rafe's.

"In some ways you're right about that." That surprised him. Maybe he had been wrong about her all these months. She didn't back down, was stronger than he'd expected, everything Darlene hadn't been. It still didn't mean she should be left to pick up the pieces if something happened to her man.

It gave him something to think about, instead of what she'd look like without any clothes on, while they went over the whole deck. Nothing stood out, but they hadn't set sail yet. That would happen in about two hours. Rafe and Murph would show up sometime tomorrow evening or the next morning, depending on when the Coast Guard got them here. Until then, they'd see what they could uncover, and he'd do his best to keep her safe and out of trouble.

For the next couple of hours they checked out three of the decks, making small talk and taking photos with their phones. They'd upload them to her laptop when they got back to their cabin. Every so often, they'd stop and take a photo together, or a drink from one of the bar carts they passed. When the ship pulled out to sea, they stood at the railing to watch along with the other passengers.

Ryan tried hard to relax into his role and not be as tied up in knots. His brain said this was a mission, but it sure as hell didn't feel like one. Then there was Chrissy. Every time she brushed against him and he got a whiff of her scent it killed him, in a good way. His mouth watered for a taste, his fingers tingled for a touch, but she seemed oblivious. Not that he thought he was God's gift to women, but something?

After exploring decks six, seven and eight, they headed back downstairs to deck five and walked around before heading to their cabin. They hadn't seen anything out of place. Used to action and danger, he wished they'd find something, someone. But it was only the first afternoon. They had the whole trip ahead of them. As she kept reminding him, there hadn't been any incidents until the return leg of the cruises. He hoped he could get through it without doing something he'd be sorry for later.

By the time they returned to the cabin, it was time for his next check in. Instead of the coms, they were using text messages at pre-arranged rendezvous times.

"I'm going to check in, then we can upload my photos."

"Okay, I'll work on mine in the meantime. I really was hoping we'd find something."

"Me too. I'm sure if there's something on this ship it will be on one of the lower decks, either in the engine room or crew quarters. Getting access will be the tricky part."

"Isn't that what Murph and Rafe are going to do?"

"Yes, but we need to try to get as much intel as possible before hand, just in case they can't get on board for some reason. It's why we have back up plans."

"Right, that makes sense."

"Jake spoke to Tex this morning. We think they realize they're being investigated."

"How? I was careful."

"But you weren't the only one looking. Tex said that the Coast Guard was working with the CIA and Homeland because of the suspicious accidents. But they didn't put it together. This is all due to you. It's why so many missions go sideways."

"That's fucked up. What's the point of the intel if it's bad or they blow the surprise?"

"I've asked myself plenty of times. But it is what it is."

"Guess so. It sucks that you have to work that way."

"We pretty much expect something to implode when we're out there."

"Okay, changing the subject a bit. I like Tex. Meghan to me that he and his family are coming to visit in the spring. I hope I get to when they're here."

"I haven't met him in person either. Hopefully we'll all get to meet them."

"We need to go head-to-head in an information hunt. I'd love to challenge him to a test to see who can come up with the most intel first. Maybe we can have a small wager."

"I did't realize you liked to bet."

"Only on sure things."

Ryan laughed harder than he had in months. She was something else and whether she liked it or not, definitely a little hellion.

"It wasn't that funny."

"Maybe," he said, still chuckling as he sent a text to Jake.

"Is everyone okay?"

"Yeah. Cam, Halo, and Jake landed at fourteen hundred. Tex is trying to dig up information about the dockings in Puerto Rico."

"Good. I didn't have a chance to take a deep dive there. But I found out a lot about the Island Sun Cruises and the shell company in Turkey who owns them. I'm still following the trail to see where that leads."

"Can you work here?"

"Yeah. It's safe with the satellite phone as the hotspot. It was too risky to use the ship's Wi-Fi."

"More James Bond toys."

"Something like that."

"I'm missing my toys. We need to locate the package on deck three."

"If you can't find it, then what?"

"Plan B, raid one of the kitchens. Knives work well and are silent."

"True."

"That reminds me, why Krav Maga? It's pretty intense for just self-defense."

"It's *very* intense. It takes focus and dedication like all martial arts, but also something more, and I needed to prove to myself that I had it."

"What made you feel that way?"

"Nothing worth talking about. It's all in the past."

"If you change your mind, I'm a good listener." Chrissy stared at him intently, her dark brown eyes like pools of melted chocolate. Lovely and unreadable. There had to be something behind that story, and he'd try to uncover it, but not now. Their mission came first.

"Maybe, but don't hold your breath, Pooky." The endearment broke the tension. He smiled and she smiled back. "We need to get through all of this before dinner. I was thinking too, we should try to arrange to have dinner with the captain."

"They do that? Wouldn't their time be better spent commanding the ship?"

"Probably. But I saw it in the brochure. I'd like to ask him a few questions, wouldn't you?"

"Fuck yeah."

CHAPTER 9

The first day at sea aboard the Jewel started like the photo from the website. Smooth sailing, lots of sunny skies, and the smiling faces of the crew. Too bad it drove Ryan out of his freaking mind. Impatience and frustration got him up and running his ten miles on the deck a little after dawn.

They'd gone to the Welcome Cocktail Party in the patio area near the pool on the sixth deck. He'd expected them to have names, but apparently whoever designed this ship didn't have an imagination. Yeah, he was cranky and tired. Instead of sleeping, he'd listened to the soft sounds of Chrissy's breathing while wishing he was making her scream his name and seeing stars. But instead, he was stretched out on the floor by himself.

As he circled the deck for the third time while listening to Ozzy, his phone buzzed with a text message. Pulling the phone from his armband, he typed in his passcode.

Jake: *No go with the Coast Guard.*

Ryan: *Copy that. Reason?*

Jake: *Rescue in the other direction.*

Dammit. Now he'd be on his own with Chrissy. Thank God for back up plans.

Ryan: *Copy. Plan B?*

Jake: *Yes. They'll be rendezvousing in PR with me. Tex is on standby if needed. Check in per schedule.*

Ryan: *Copy.*

Even Ozzy couldn't fix his present mood. It shouldn't have pissed him off, but this time he had a civilian with him. Sure Chrissy was a trained FBI agent, but Krav Maga or not, she'd never been in the field.

Finishing his run, he headed to the cabin. The suite had a stocked coffee bar, and he needed a shower. As he ran past the pool he was tempted to jump in and do a few laps. It might help drain off some of his tension. But coffee and a hot shower won out.

Chrissy was sitting on the balcony when he got back. Thank God she was dressed. If she'd been wearing some kind of sexy lingerie he'd have lost control. Instead she was in shorts and a tank top. He'd never noticed how long her legs were, which made him wonder what they'd feel like wrapped around his waist or over his shoulders. Fuck.

"I'm going to grab a quick shower, be right out."

"Okay, and good morning."

He didn't answer just grabbed something out of the drawer to wear and closed the bathroom door. Get a grip, asshole. She probably thought he was upset with her. Or not. He had no idea what the woman was thinking. Maybe if he did, this wouldn't suck so much. For over a year he'd kept his attraction contained, but one fucking day with her and he was hornier than a fifteen year old jerking off to computer porn.

Standing under the ice cold water, he hoped it would cool down his raging libido. He really was a fucktard. The cold shower did the trick, and after he was calmer, he finished washing up and even shaved. By the time he stepped out of the bathroom he was a new, calmer, Ryan. How long it would last, was a whole other issue.

"I made you some coffee. Black with two sugars, right?"

"Yes, thank you. I'm surprised you remembered."

"It's my thing." That was the closest she'd come to admitting to him she had amazing skills.

"Cool. Your 'thing' can make me coffee anytime."

"Did you sleep at all?"

"A little. How about you?"

"Not much, maybe an hour or two. Something is bothering me."

"About the mission?"

"Yes, and no. It's the information from Tex. Why would Homeland know about this? We haven't found a credible threat. I know the director didn't tell them. It's a joint mission with the Navy and they read in the NSA. Not that they needed to. I'm sure they knew everything as soon as I wrote my first report."

"Probably."

"Anyway, I keep trying to figure out why the Coast Guard would pull in Homeland. All they did was help ensure a disabled ship made it into port.

"Good point. Let's give it a couple of hours and then give Tex a call and see if he's turned up anything else."

"I've been digging around, but I haven't found anything."

"There's other news, too," Ryan said as he pulled a deck chair near the table. "Jake texted already. There's been a change of plan and Rafe and Murph are on their way to Puerto Rico."

"What? Did something happen?"

"I'm not sure. It sounds fishy. Their ship got a distress call miles in the opposite direction."

"I suppose it could be a real call but you're right, definitely fishy."

"It means we're on our own and we have to find my weapons package asap. The rest of the team will be in Puerto Rico looking for information and hopefully their hiding place. I'm betting they find a weapons stash."

"I hope I'm wrong, but I don't think so. As for here, we can handle it." Her comment didn't surprise him. But if it turned into a shit show, his first priority would be to keep her safe.

"I don't want any more surprises. We have to

figure a way to get to the lower decks without being seen."

"I've been thinking about that too. I found a copy of the ship's schematics on line. If there is a way to get below without being seen, we'll find it on these plans."

"How long have you been awake?"

"Since you went to run. I thought about joining you, but I don't like running. I'd rather sit by the pool and be lazy."

"You're funny."

"Thank you. You're not so bad yourself."

"Wow, that's high praise from the hellion." She stuck her tongue out. As tempted as he was to swoop in and kiss her, he stayed in his chair and took a long drink of coffee instead.

"What's our plan for today?"

"We keep doing what we started yesterday. Explore deck by deck and see how far below we can get before we're stopped."

"Okay. Oh yeah, something else. I put in a request for us to have dinner with the captain tonight. We should hear by lunch if we were selected."

"Selected?"

"Yeah, it's a lottery system or something. I don't get it. But with any luck we'll be chosen."

"Maybe we should see if Tex can make sure we are."

"Umm, if you think that's a good idea?"

"Yeah. I can't believe that the captain of any ship wouldn't know everything going on."

"I think so too. You think you can get him to talk about it?"

"We'll see. I could if I got him alone, but not sure if I can with as many people around, as there will be at dinner."

"It just means we have to be smarter than him. Or catch him off guard."

"I need more coffee, are you ready for another?"

"Yes, please, two sugars and a..."

"You don't have to tell me. I'm observant too." Ryan stepped through the sliding doors carrying their mugs and made them each a fresh cup. At some point fresh muffins had been dropped off and he carried them out to the balcony. "Look what I found."

"Oh yeah, I forgot to tell you. I ordered them after you left. I figured you'd be hungry when you got back." She'd gotten them for him? He could almost hear his father's voice telling him not to be an ass. But then he saw Darlene's face, her pain, and how the loss affected all of them.

"I appreciate it, but you don't have to take care of me."

"You're welcome. Don't be an ass. I was just making sure you didn't wake the whole ship up with your growly belly."

"If you say so."

"I do, now eat your muffin like a good Pooky." After she said it she ducked, but he still hit her with one of the muffins. She caught it before it hit the deck and took a big bite. "Yummy. Thank you." And went right back to whatever she was doing on the laptop without missing a beat.

As Chrissy stared at the laptop screen, she needed to get a grip before she jumped on him and ripped off his clothes. She had it bad. Meghan would laugh her ass off if she could see her now. What would he say if she initiated the sex discussion? They were adults. A little casual sex never hurt anyone. Except she knew damn well that wasn't all she wanted no matter how much she'd fought it.

They'd known each other for almost a year and spent most of that time sniping at each other. And now the universe decides this is when she needs to take a chance on a relationship. With a SEAL no less. Could she ask for worse relationship material? Sure, Megan and Miranda made it work, but she wasn't like them. She saw all the variables for everything that happened, every argument, every everything. Who'd want a relationship with someone like her? It was the reason she'd avoided them all these years. Too bad her heart wasn't listening to her.

"Did you find something?"

"Huh, no. Why?"

"Because you're staring at the screen like it grew a new head." She'd thought he was eating his muffins and ignoring her. Of course he wasn't.

"I was thinking, sorry. I work things out in my mind a lot. I know it's kind of weird."

"I know."

"What?"

"Jake gave me your file. He thought it was

important that I know since we were going to be working together on this."

"Now I know why you've been different. You think I'm a freak, right?"

"No, how could you think that? I think you're amazing. That your brain can do all that stuff. Shit. I'm jealous."

She'd avoided looking at him but turned to face him, to read his expression, his eyes. Was he telling the truth, or just saying what he figured she'd want to hear? They still had a mission to complete.

"Really?" She hated how pitiful she sounded. Like a wounded bird. This is why she kept it to herself.

"Yes, Chrissy. You're not a freak. Fuck, you have the closest thing to super powers that exist in the real world."

She'd never looked at it like that. He was still looking her in the face, he hadn't turned away, hadn't made fun of her, there was even something in his eyes, something she couldn't quite decipher.

"Woman, if you keep looking at me like that, you're not going to like the results."

"Huh?"

"Like you're waiting to get punched."

"I guess in a way I am. Not literally just verbally." She'd expected to get pity, but he surprised her again. Instead of talking, he pulled her onto his lap.

"I'm going to kiss you. If you don't want me to, say no now." Dumbfounded she just sat there. Kiss her? Hell yeah. Bring it on big guy. Except she couldn't make her mouth move, couldn't form the words. And then it happened. The kiss she'd dreamed about for months, fantasized about.

Gentle at first, when she didn't pull away, he pulled her closer, and slid his tongue between her lips. He tasted like coffee and carrot muffins and heat. Sighing into his mouth, she slid her tongue against his, sucking it further in. She felt alive for the first time, her body tingled from the top of her head to her toes. And then it was over.

"What the fuck?" He sounded breathless, hoarse.

"Is that how you always react to a kiss?" she asked as she tried to get up.

"No. But wow. I did not expect that."

"Good or bad?"

"How can you even ask? Dammit, woman.

You come across all tough and self-confident but it's mostly an act isn't it?"

"Umm, do we have to talk about this now? I'd much rather we go make use of the bed in the other room. Unless you're not interested."

"Not interested? Shit. I'll show you who's not interested." He stood with her still in his arms like she weighed nothing and carried her to the bed. She half expected he'd drop her, but he put her down gently, then walked away.

"Where are you going?"

"To put the Do Not Disturb sign on the door. I'd prefer to enjoy you in private."

She didn't need to see her face to know it was flaming. She was hot and cold all at the same time. It had been at least six years since she'd had sex. Would he be disappointed? Would she? Her thoughts were flying, analyzing everything she was thinking about.

"Stop it."

"Stop what?"

"Stop overthinking. Just let it happen. You don't have to work this out, it will take care of itself. I promise."

She stared at him. Where had this man come from. This was the man of her dreams, but how could he be so different from the Ryan she'd known all these months?

"You're doing it again. Do we need to talk about this first? Will that help you relax?"

"No, maybe, fuck. I don't know."

"Okay, that means yes. Do you want to talk here or go sit on the couch?"

"Here's fine. I'm sorry, I guess I could ruin a wet dream, huh? I'm sure you have a case of blue balls by now."

He howled with laughter and her first instinct was to hide, but he wasn't laughing at her. "I have been walking around with them, practically since the day we met. It's only gotten worse over time."

"Then why are you so obnoxious to me all the time?"

"I could ask you the same thing. But, I guess I need to apologize. It's how I keep people at arm's length. Sarcasm. It's safer that way."

"Yes, it definitely is. Why do you keep people away? You know my reason."

"Are you upset I know?"

"Yes, no, maybe? I don't know. I try to keep it hidden. Being different sucks. I've spent most of my life trying to hide from it."

"I'm sorry. People can be cruel. I guess I was one of those people."

"Yes, but not you. You were just Mr. Pissy Pants."

"Geesh. And you thought hellion was bad? Mr. Pissy Pants?"

"Yeah. Looks like women are a lot better at keeping secrets from their men than the other way around."

"I guess so."

"Why did you try so hard to get me to hate you?"

"Probably for the same reason you did. I didn't want to be attracted to you. Didn't want the distraction…"

"That's not all of it."

"No it's not, but I'm not sure that now is the right time for this discussion."

She was going to object, but his phone buzzed.

CHAPTER 10

Ryan pulled out his phone and opened the encrypted message. Another update from Jake. "Fuck. Turns out we were wrong. The CIA brought in the Coasties and they notified Homeland."

"Why the hell would they do that?" The sparkle in her eyes and playfulness evaporated as his words sank in. Chrissy could compartmentalize faster than anyone he'd ever met.

"Because there's a chemical weapon on board or will be."

"No way. I haven't seen any chatter about anything bio or chemical," Chrissy said.

"It's good intel."

"You're sure about that?"

Ryan hesitated. How much could he tell her? He knew the chemist was bad news as soon as he'd seen the slimy bastard. Deciding as senior man in the field, okay, only man in the field, he'd read her in on most of it. "The CIA has a Russian chemist stashed somewhere and they're wringing information out of him. He was working on a slow release remote activated delivery system for the VX."

"Holy shit balls. All of that was in the text?"

"Not all of it, some of it I already knew."

Chrissy nodded. "Gotcha, prior mission stuff. What else can you tell me?"

"The CIA grabbed the owner of the cruise line yesterday after the chemist spilled his guts. He's a total fucking scumbag." As he spoke, he watched Chrissy's reactions. At the first mention of the VX gas the color drained out of her face but was her only outward reaction.

"I'd have to agree with that assessment. Do we know where it is?"

"No. All Nechayev told them was the weapon and three men were boarding this ship and taking it in through Puerto Rico. At least, that's all he's admitted so far. If he's right, they're not on the ship yet."

"It confirms my theory, though."

"Yes, it does."

"They'll be boarding at our first port of call. I knew I was missing a piece of the puzzle."

"What do you mean?" Ryan asked.

"I couldn't figure out why this had escalated over the last couple of months. Something had changed to make them speed up their process. It made it more obvious when they had to make so many emergency stops in Puerto Rico."

"And now you know why?"

"Yes, because today we dock in Nassau."

"I don't understand? What's special about Nassau?"

"The Bahamas were decimated by Hurricane Dorian. They're taking aid from everywhere. It's easy to show up to help then travel to the other islands in the archipelago. They'd only do a cursory document check. Nassau took in a lot of refugees from the islands hit hardest, and they are overwhelmed."

"Fuck me running," Ryan said and sent an encrypted message to Jake and Tex.

"They're still pulling dead bodies out of the rubble on Abaco. It's so sad what happened, and these assholes are using the disaster to their advantage."

"It doesn't surprise me. These jihadists don't care about anything but the cause. I've seen them put a vest on their child and blow them up to take out a table of marines in a café."

"Not on my watch," Chrissy said, the resolve dripping from her words. Her eyes were like brown marbles, hard and glowing with anger.

"We'll get them. But first we have to figure out who they are."

"I'd bet most passengers won't go ashore. Unless they want to volunteer, there is nothing else for them to do on the island."

"How many ways off and on the ship in port?" Ryan asked as he two-finger typed into his phone.

Chrissy got the map of the ship and spread it out on the bed. He almost smiled when he realized she was doing that for him, she already knew. "There's one for passengers and one for the crew to load or offload supplies. We're lucky it's a small ship."

Ryan nodded, typed in the rest of the info, and clicked send. He expected his phone to ring any second and he wasn't wrong.

"I sent it to Tex and Jake. Maybe Tex can get access to something you can't."

"Good idea. I was going to suggest that. The more eyes we have the better. They can't get off this ship with the gas."

Before he could answer her, the phone rang. Ryan pushed the speaker button so Chrissy could hear.

"Jake, you're on speaker."

"Good work. Maybe we'll get a break on this one. Will you be able to cover both access points?"

Ryan said, "No." But Chrissy answered yes.

"Do we have a problem?"

"No." This time they answered in unison.

"I don't like this either, Ryan, but we need to use *all* of our resources."

"Yes, Boss."

"Did you locate the weapon package on deck three?"

"Negative. It's not a passenger deck, and I haven't been able to get down there. I tried this morning during my run but was turned back twice. I'll have it before we dock this afternoon."

"You are to locate and report only. Do not engage. I repeat do not engage until we have confirmation of all HVTs. The last thing we need is VX gas being released on that ship."

"Copy that. Anything else?"

"We located their nest in Puerto Rico and we have it staked out to see what pops up."

"That's great," Chrissy said.

"Yeah, Tex found a recent purchase of a warehouse that matched up with the shell company."

"It's good they're not as smart as they think they are."

"Oh they're smart but not as good as you and Tex," Jake replied. "Stick to the encrypted texts until you hear different. Good luck and Chrissy be careful."

"Only me? What about Ryan?"

"I already know he's careful. I don't know how you'll react. It's not a slight just a warning."

"Yes, sir."

Ryan slid the phone back into his pocket and waited for the explosion. It didn't happen. "You're not pissed off?"

"Why? Because you said we couldn't cover the access points? You're trying to protect me. I'd be an ass for being mad about that? I am perfectly capable of taking care of myself, please trust me."

"I'm trying."

"Try harder," she said with a smile. "I'm hungry are there any muffins left?"

"You're hungry now?"

"Yes, what's wrong with that?"

"Nothing," he said and shook his head as he checked the coffee bar for muffins. He grabbed two and checked the mini-fridge and grabbed the bowl of grapes. "Will this work?"

"Perfect," she answered from behind him. Damn, he hadn't heard her, and only picked up a whiff of her scent seconds before she answered him. "I'll meet you at the table."

It was oh seven hundred, they still had six hours before the ship docked in Nassau. Six hours to plan out how they would proceed. Chrissy was at the laptop, her fingers flying over the keys. Putting the food on the counter, he set up another pot of coffee. They were definitely going to need it.

Maybe she should have been annoyed. If it had happened last week, she'd have bitten his head off and fed it to him. Funny how quickly things can change. After the evening at Meghan's she'd gotten a better idea of the real Ryan he'd kept hidden. Then these last couple of days being around him constantly really opened her eyes. He was hiding from pain of a severe loss. Not a weird ability that people freaked out from, like she was, his was some kind of heartbreak and he'd built a brick wall around himself. She didn't know what had happened, but she could read people and if she was wrong she'd go for a run on the beach with him.

Then there was that kiss. He'd curled her toes and made her woman parts sit up and say hell yeah. If they hadn't been interrupted, she'd probably have needed to be resuscitated. Turns out Mr. Pissy Pants had a super power too, the ability to turn her into a drooling female craving his touch after one kiss. Wowzah.

"I made coffee." Ryan put a fresh cup near her hand along with a couple of muffins and some grapes.

"Bless you. Coffee is my spirit animal."

"You're a little crazy, you know that?"

"Oh yeah, believe me I've heard it all."

"No, I didn't mean it that way. Geesh, prickly. I wasn't lying when I said I'm jealous of your abilities. You don't have to hide them from me."

Tilting her head to the side, she scoured his face for any indication he was lying but it wasn't there, and no pity either. The eyes that met hers held no secrets and she melted.

She needed to focus. There were lives in danger. Pulling her gaze away from his eyes, it dropped to his lips. She could still feel his lips against hers, how he tasted as she slid her tongue along his. Damn. *Christine Stillwell, you need to get your act together, damp panties or not.*

"Thank you. I'll try but no promises. It will definitely make this mission easier."

"Exactly. So tell me what I can do to help?" Ryan said as he pulled his chair closer to hers to see the laptop screen.

Focus.

Focus.

Focus.

Closing her eyes for a moment to clear the vision she had of the two of them in bed, she grabbed the coffee and took a huge gulp. They had excellent coffee on this cruise, she'd give them that.

"Deck three has the employee access. See here?" She zoomed the screen to show him the location. "Since it's on the same deck as the weapon package, are you going to take that one?"

"Yeah, that's what I was thinking. With any luck, two of the three will come in that way with the gas. I'm not sure how big it is."

"Right." Expanding another window on the laptop, there were several different options she'd found for the VX container. "It could be in anything like these. Probably like this backpack. Or that case."

"How much damage can that do if released?"

Chrissy sat back in the chair and visualized the question, sliding through scenarios as quickly as they appeared. Wind speed and location were the determining factors. "Not much, but it depends on how it's released. As an example, if it's released into the air vents of this ship, we'd be dead by the time the Coast Guard answered our SOS."

"Fuck. And if it gets home?"

"Again it depends Do we know if it's only one device or have they already brought over others?"

"That we don't know. If the CIA is aware they're not sharing at the moment."

"Not a surprise. What is though, is that

they're not dropping someone into the mix to take over. We're in international waters, they wouldn't be breaking any rules."

"Jake wondered that too. He has Tex verifying that there are no agents aboard. We don't need any surprises."

"No shit.

"Where will you be?" Ryan asked as he leaned into the laptop and reached for the mouse..

"Hey, hands off, Pooky. No touchy." Chrissy smacked his hand. "This is mine, you should have brought your own."

"Damn. That's not very nice. We are married, what's yours is mine, and vice versa," Ryan said as he rubbed his hand, pretending to be injured.

"Nice try, but no. If one little slap causes you that much pain, how the hell did you become a SEAL?"

He laughed. "Touché."

"Stop messing around now, we need to figure this out before we dock. Plus you need time to figure out how to get to deck three and find your guns."

"Yes, ma'am. I apologize for the distraction."

"Here's the passenger disembarkation point.

I'll have to hang around there or get off and watch from the island."

"I'd prefer you stay on board. If they make you, it'll be easier to hide on the ship than it would be on the island right now."

"Agreed. So we both stay on board, right?"

He hesitated for a few beats then nodded in agreement. Pulling away from his gaze, she brought up deck three on the screen again.

"I think the panel will be here, do you have a small screwdriver to remove the screws?"

"No, but they'd have known that, and left it open for me."

"I don't know, it's the FBI not another SEAL team. Hold on," she got up and went to her purse. Pulling out her small travel manicure set, she removed the file. It would work as long as it wasn't screwed in too tightly.

"This might work." Handing him the nail file she sat down and popped a grape into her mouth and chewed. "Oh, these are good. Try one."

Reaching for the bowls, she popped one into his mouth. "Mmmm. Delicious."

The way his eyes glittered as he said it, made her wonder if they were still talking about grapes.

"I'll be here. The Patio Lounge is right there. I'll be able to sit, and people watch, and no one will be any wiser."

"Good. If I don't have to worry about you, I'll be able to concentrate more."

"I keep telling you..."

"Yes, I know." This time he popped a grape into her mouth to shut her up.

"Fine," she said after she swallowed. "Next question. What are we going to do when we find it?"

"We'll secure it on the ship and then hand it over to the CDC guys."

"You think it'll be that simple?"

"I sure hope so. As for the guys, they won't be a problem."

"Pretty sure of yourself, aren't you?"

"I eat bad guys for breakfast."

"No you don't, you ate pumpkin muffins." She enjoyed surprising him. He probably spent a lot of time rescuing women who could barely handle themselves let alone anything else. But she didn't need saving.

"I didn't see that coming."

"Hopefully that's the only thing that gets by you today."

"I thought you said you didn't do well around people."

"Nope, I said I didn't around people *I don't know*. I know you pretty damn well."

"Are you flirting with me?"

"Maybe?"

"In the middle of planning a mission?"

"It's planned, we just have a few details to work out. They're not on board yet, we have a few hours before the shit hits the fan, so what's wrong with a little teasing?"

"Aren't you worried?"

"No, I don't have time for that and you're a hard ass Navy SEAL. They won't know what hit them."

"Pretty sure of yourself."

"I'm confident in my skills and that makes me positive about you. Everything about you screams protector. You'll do anything to make sure no one gets hurt.

CHAPTER 11

The Jewel docked in Nassau an hour earlier. Chrissy was in place to surveil the public access on deck six. So far so good. They'd had several com checks since then. Ryan left first, since he had to get down to deck three.

After mapping three options with Chrissy, he opted to try the second option and was able to get onto the deck and locate the weapon package almost immediately. The nail file worked on the screws, since she'd been correct, and they were all in place.

The stash left for him contained two Sigs and a Ka-Bar knife. *Perfect*. He finally felt mission ready. The last day had been the first time in probably fifteen years that he'd spent a whole day without being armed.

"Sit rep?" Ryan whispered into his coms.

"All clear."

"Copy that." When he gave her the com equipment, along with a quick demo, he stressed that she could whisper, and he'd hear her. The last thing he wanted was her to put herself in danger while answering him.

This was Ryan's least favorite part of his job. Surveillance was tedious any way he looked at it. Alone it was worse, especially if the location didn't get a lot of use. Since he'd settled into his spot, there had been five large pallets of supplies that left the ship. The same crew members had returned empty-handed each time.

Two hours down and three to go before they pulled anchor. If he had to wager a guess, the HVTs would come aboard just before undocking. It's what he'd do.

"I landed a live one," Chrissy said over the com.

"Copy that. How many tangos?"

"One big one, carrying," she answered.

Fuck. He'd hoped that they'd bring it in

through the crew access point. But now they'd have to watch for both.

"Copy that."

"Sending you a pic," she whispered.

Those glasses of hers were really handy especially for surveillance missions like this. He didn't know how she was able to send from them, but after this was all over, he'd see if Jake could get a few pairs for the team.

"Copy and received." Ryan had his phone in his hand to view the image as soon as it was delivered. A photo of a short, middle eastern man, wearing beige slacks, a floral button-down shirt, and carrying a small black bag appeared on his phone. He blended in with the passengers in the image except for his face. The others were smiling and chatting with their companions. His expression was dour, and his grip was so tight on the bag that his knuckles were white. If it wasn't the VX, it was equally as important and possibly dangerous.

"I sent it to my boss to run," she whispered.

"Copy. What's he doing now?"

"He's sitting two tables away. It looks like he's waiting for someone."

"Okay. If he moves, you move, but keep your distance. I'm still clear here."

"Copy. But you don't have to remind me. I know what to do."

"Chrissy…" He couldn't hide the strain in his voice. Leaving her alone and in danger was against everything he believed in. It didn't matter that she believed she was safe and could protect herself. Maybe he was a macho asshole, but he still believed in keeping women and children safe no matter what.

"Slow your roll there, Pooky. I'm being good."

That's what worried him, and he was about to tell her that, when he had movement. Two men dressed in uniforms walked through the doorway. They did a better job than the man Chrissy had tagged. These two were casual, chatted and looked like they belonged there. But they didn't. He'd been there since they'd lowered the gangway and they'd never gotten off. They had to be the two tangos. Snapping a photo with his phone, he sent it to Tex, Jake, and Chrissy.

"Chrissy, I've got the other two."

"Okay. We might have a problem," she whispered back.

The words sent Ryan's stomach into a tailspin. "What's up?" He tried to sound calm, but he was far from it. Even if he hadn't had feelings for her, he'd have been worried. She had no backup and was unarmed.

"My friend has a visitor in an officer's uniform."

Fuck. He shouldn't have been surprised. It made the most sense. Even the worst managed ship had someone overseeing everything. There had to be a person telling the crew to look the other way when strangers showed up.

"Can you get a photo of the officer?"

"Not at the moment. His back is to me."

"Copy that. Don't put yourself in jeopardy." She didn't answer. He told himself she didn't want to be overheard. Chrissy had planned to bring her tablet to seem like she was reading and order coffee at the Patio Bar. It was a good cover, but nothing was perfect.

A half hour later he'd followed the two fake crew members to their quarters. If they didn't come out soon he was going to have to move, ships weren't built with hiding places in passageways. He had gotten close enough to clone one of the HVT's phones. It wouldn't give him much if they didn't make a call, but it was better than nothing.

"Sit rep, Chrissy." Again no answer. He didn't like it. She knew to respond unless it was dangerous. But she should be sitting out in the open having coffee. Unless her tango was on the move. Even then she was on passenger decks. He was a heartbeat away from texting Tex to see if he could track her phone, when she answered.

"Stop worrying. I'm fine."

"Why didn't you answer?"

"We were all going for a walk. My guy is very antsy. He and the officer went for a walk around the deck. I couldn't get close enough to overhear their discussion, but I did keep him in sight."

"Where are you now?"

"In our cabin. Guess who is right next door? Talk about luck, huh? And I pegged him with a tracker when I passed him at his door."

Ryan didn't know what to say at first. He was hoping his cloned phone would pay off, and she got a tracker on her HVT. "Excellent job. I didn't know you had trackers."

"I didn't either until I opened the little case where they'd packed the chargers for all my equipment. They were stashed in the headphone case. Do you want me to come find you so we can tag your guys?"

"You're enjoying this aren't you?"

"Is that bad? I know this is dangerous and it's not a game, but I can't help it. I know I'm weird, but this is everything I thought working for the FBI would be."

Listening to her explanation reminded him of his first few SEAL missions and he could totally relate. After years of dealing with really bad guys, the shine had worn off. "No, it's not bad. But you can't let your guard down."

"I don't intend to. Now, do you want me to bring you a couple of trackers?"

"As long as you won't lose your tango."

"I won't. Where are you?"

Of course he made it more difficult explaining where he was, instead of just telling her his location, completely forgetting she'd know it from location. It would take some getting used to having a girlfriend with super powers.

"Okay, I'll see you asap."

While he waited for her, he tossed the word around. Girlfriend, it sounded weird coming out of his mouth or even in his thoughts. Just because they were getting along on this, didn't mean it would work long term. Did he even want to go down that path?

Expecting to see Chrissy in the passageway any moment, he checked the quarters for his two tangos. He could hear arguing inside, or at least it sounded like an argument, but he couldn't hear the words. Then his phone buzzed.

Pulling it out, he thought it would be Jake, but the text message was in Arabic. His clone worked, but his reading skills weren't as good. He was much better at Pashto based on where they spent most of their time. He'd have to forward these on for translation. It was too important to fuck it up.

While in the process of forwarding it to Jake, Chrissy appeared at the end of the passageway. "Is it safe to approach?"

"Yes. But if a door opens, keep walking and act like you're lost."

"Copy that."

They didn't have to worry about it, she was able to hand off the trackers without incident.

"Thank you. Go back to the cabin. I forwarded a text to Jake for translation. I'll wait here for these fuckers to come out so I can tag them."

"Did they have a case too?"

"No."

"Be careful, Pooky. You're growing on me. I'd hate to lose you already."

"You're hysterical. I'm more worried about you right now. Remember your HVT has the gas."

"I know," she answered as she headed down the passageway. Just before she was out of sight, she blew him a kiss. What was he going to do with her? His libido answered, make her come until she can't breathe and then some more. The thought of her writhing underneath him, her body flushed, her voice husky as she moaned his name, made him rock hard.

It disappeared instantly when he heard a door open. Turning his back, he stood at one of the doors as if trying to get inside. The crew member walked by without paying him any attention. *Fucking idiot.*

What was she thinking blowing Ryan a kiss?

They're in the middle of a mission that could cost people their lives, thousands of people, and she was acting like a lovesick teenager. Wait? Love? Where did that come from?

Kicking herself in the virtual butt, she shook her head and concentrated on the mission. Her HVT was still in his cabin according to one of the little blinking lights on her phone. The other was right where she'd left him, in the passageway. Maybe she should have told him she was tracking him. He was a SEAL. Except her gut told her to do it, and she never second guessed her intuition, even if it meant pissing him off when he found out.

Fifteen minutes later she was in their cabin watching little blinking blips on her tablet and pacing the suite. The waiting shit sucked. No wonder everyone complained about stake outs. Waiting at the Patio Bar wasn't bad, she could watch the other passengers come and go, drink as much iced coffee as she wanted, and occasionally talk to Ryan. But this? This sucked donkey balls. He was two decks down, and she was up there hoping Mr. Terrorist didn't get an itchy trigger finger.

Just when she was about to lose her mind, her

phone buzzed with a call. Not Ryan, he'd use the coms.

"Hello?"

"Chrissy, it's Jake. What's your status? I can't reach Ryan."

"I'm fine. In the cabin. Where are you? It sounds like you're in a factory or something, it's so loud."

"Chopper. Is everything okay?" Why was he in a chopper and where were they headed? She wanted to ask, but he was hitting her with one question after another.

"We have the HVTs under surveillance. One guy is in the cabin next door with what we think is the VX gas. Ryan is babysitting the other two. They're on deck three in crew quarters."

"How are you holding up?"

"I'm fine, except for all this waiting. I want to go in there and knock him out and take the VX away from him. Why? What's going on?"

"Sit tight for a bit longer. We're on our way."

"You're coming here? What about not alerting the HVTs?"

"They already know."

"How...oh wait, the text Ryan forwarded, right? But how did they get contacted?"

"Yes, it's why I'm trying to reach him. We need to neutralize the threat and secure the VX."

"Let me try my coms. Give me a second." She put him on mute and tried to reach Ryan. He didn't answer her either. Running over to the table, she grabbed the tablet. While she'd been on the phone, his blinking light had moved, but not much. Her gut twisted into a knot so tight she doubled over in pain. They had him, she knew it without a doubt. "I think the HVTs he was stalking got him."

"Is that your gut talking?"

"Yes, but also his tracker moved. I think he's in their quarters now."

"You put a tracker on him?"

"Yeah, because of things like this. So don't give me any shit."

"I wasn't going to. It was brilliant."

That took her by surprise, but she didn't have time to think about it. Her terrorist was on the move. "Fuck. Jake, I have to go. My terrorist just left his cabin, and I think he's headed toward Ryan's location."

"Chrissy, sit tight. We'll be there in about fifteen minutes."

"What if Ryan doesn't have that much time? What if they're going to use the gas on the ship?"

"Ryan knew what he was getting into, he's a SEAL. But..."

"Bye, Jake. I'll text you his location. See you when you get here."

She'd be damned if she was going to stay in her room and not do anything. There were hundreds of passengers and crew on this ship. She'd sworn an oath, and she meant it.

After sending the text with Ryan's location, she changed her flip flops to sneakers, and took a knife from the kitchenette and tucked it into her waistband. Grabbing the tablet, she followed the blinking lights. As she moved down the passageway to the first set of stairs, she whispered, "Ryan, hold on, Pooky. I'm coming for you."

She should have checked the cabin next door to see if the terrorist left the black bag behind, but she wouldn't have let it out of her sight, so he probably hadn't either. Her guess about where he was headed was correct. He'd just entered the passageway on deck three. It would be another twelve minutes, if Jake was right about their arrival time, but then they had to get to deck three.

Once she was on deck three, she took off at a run. The feeling that every second counted, haunted her as she made her way down the passageway. The two blinking lights were next to each other. Shit balls.

CHAPTER 12

Chrissy stood outside the door looking at the two blinking lights on the other side. There were at least four voices in there, but the door was too thick to make out what they were saying or even what language they were speaking.

It was decision time. Out of all the scenarios she'd come up with, she'd narrowed it down to three options that might work. First option: Activate the fire alarm and hope they come out. Second option: Call the ship's security and ask for help. That her husband was missing, and she'd tracked him to that location with her phone. Third option: knock on the door, play helpless female, and take them by surprise.

The first she discarded immediately. The second was doable, but the third would be her best shot. If she'd had more time she might have come up with a better plan, but all of her instincts screamed go now. Ditching the tablet down the passageway, she got out her phone and pulled up the location app as part of her cover.

After taking a deep breath, she knocked on the door. The voices on the other side were instantly quiet. She knocked again and called out with her best southern belle impersonation. "I know my husband is in there. You may not know he's married, but darlin' you don't want him. Bless your heart. We're on this cruise to celebrate and he's off with you. Now you let me in, right now."

The door swung open. Chrissy expected her terrorist to be on the other side, not a ship's officer.

"Mrs. Bennett, is it?"

"Why, yes it is. How are you? Is my husband here? His phone says he is. We're on this cruise to fix our marriage. Wait until daddy hears about this. He's gonna to rake him through the thick Georgia mud." She was going to milk this for all it was worth. His body blocked most of the doorway and she couldn't see around him.

"I'm the ship's safety officer, Armin Reza. And yes, he's here."

"Oh my, thank goodness. The lyin' cheatin' dog." She wasn't sure that Reza was buying her act, but until she knew she was fucked, she'd keep it up. Every second she kept him busy bought them more time.

"I think you have your husband all wrong."

"Really? I highly doubt it, he's been sowin' his seeds all over the county for years. This was his last chance."

Reza took a step back so she could enter. Steeling her mind for whatever she would see next, she wanted to cry when she saw Ryan. They had him restrained and beat him until he was a bloody mes.

"What have you done to him? You're a brute. How dare you hurt him." Pushing past him, she ran to Ryan's side hoping he was still alive.

"Your husband isn't who you think he is, Mrs. Barrett. What I don't know is are you also not who you profess to be?"

"Me? What on earth? You've lost your ever lovin' mind. Wait till I tell my daddy how this cruise line treated us. You'll be out of business before..."

The punch took her by surprise, left her breathless and knocked her to her knees. Chrissy hadn't noticed the other man behind Reza. Stupid. Letting the tears run down her cheeks, she didn't have to try too hard to look shocked and confused.

"What's wrong with you people?"

"I think you need to be quiet, unless you want to end up like your husband."

Still kneeling on the floor, tears sliding down her cheeks, she closed her eyes for a moment to get a clearer picture of the room. That's when she heard it. A faint sound. It was Ryan, barely breathing words into his coms so the HVTs wouldn't realize he was awake.

"I'm okay."

Thank God.

Muslim men thought women were worthless, except for bearing children, so she wasn't surprised when they turned their backs on her and spoke in rapid Arabic. It gave her the opportunity to cut the duct tape on Ryan's wrists and give him the knife. There were four bad guys and the two of them, but they still had half a chance, as long as they didn't set off the VX gas.

Chrissy wanted to kick their terrorist asses, but the thought of the VX stopped her. They needed a plan, right now, and it had to work. One of the men turned to look at her. She kept her head bowed and continued to sniffle. The longer they thought she was helpless the better.

Reza said something to him in Arabic and he left the cabin. Where was he going? She hadn't seen the bag with the VX. Maybe they'd already set it release on the ship. He could be getting their exit confirmed.

Time stood still once she'd entered the room. The Black Eagles could already be on the ship or they might still be in the chopper. They needed a plan. Glancing around the room, she located the black bag on the bottom bunk about six feet from her. If it was still in the room, she felt confident they hadn't decided to use it on the ship. At least not yet. Could she get to it before they realized what she was doing? She gave herself a fifty-fifty chance, maybe sixty-forty, but those odds weren't good enough. It would be a disaster if she failed. They needed a diversion.

Not sure how badly Ryan was injured, she

had to get him and the VX out of that room to neutralize the threat. Chrissy was about to go for it when the other guy came back with her tablet in his hand. Fuck.

Seeing the electronic device really pissed off Reza and he started screaming. That's when she knew he was in charge and had been on the ship all along. Had he decided the target for the VX too? Chrissy was itching to rip him a new one.

If she got out of this mess, she was going to learn Arabic. It sucked not knowing what they were saying. And she really wanted to understand what they planned to do next. The yelling stopped and Reza approached her.

"Woman, why are you really here? And what is this?" he asked as he held her tablet in front of her face. "We saw you earlier, and now you're here in this cabin. That's not a coincidence." It was kind of ironic, the angrier he got the thicker his accent became.

"It looks like a tablet. But I don't know what you're talking about? You saw me?"

"Don't fuck with me, bitch, or that punch will feel like a child's kiss."

Men can be such assholes. So sure of themselves. That's where Reza made his mistake. He didn't like Chrissy's answer and kicked at her while she was on the floor. It was the chance she'd been waiting for. Whispering to Ryan, she told him to move if he could. She grabbed Reza's foot and pulled him down onto the floor.

Everything moved in slow motion after that. Standing, she used the moves she'd practiced for the last three years in Krav Maga, except this time she didn't have to worry about killing anyone. If they died it would be one less terrorist in the world.

"Chrissy don't…" Ryan said through the coms.

It was too late. Reza lay on the floor his arm dislocated, his leg broken, and most likely a fractured jaw. The one HVT realized what was happening as she reached for the bag, but she was faster than he was. She had forgotten one thing—the detonator.

While she focused on him, Ryan dealt with the other two. She wanted to help but was afraid to turn her focus away from the asshole with the detonator.

"Don't do this. You'll die too."

"So be it," he said with a sneer in heavily accented English. "I will die a martyr. You'll be responsible for the deaths of all of these people."

Feeling movement next to her, she glanced to her side to see Ryan take out the second HVT and stand next to her.

"Give it to me. You don't want to die. You're only in this for the money."

"Infidel," he screamed. "You will never stop us. We'll never give up."

That was true, their hatred knew no bounds, and they twisted the words of the Koran to justify it all. But he wasn't going to win today. Not while she was still breathing. That's when she saw the porthole. If he started the activation sequence and she could get the bag into the water before it detonated, no one would have to die.

Thankfully, she didn't need to find out how fast she could move. They'd done it, stalled him long enough for the cavalry to bust through the door. She'd never been so happy to see anyone in her life.

Before the fucker realized what was happening, four very angry SEALs and a vicious dog burst through the door.

"He's got the detonator in his hand," Ryan

yelled. Halo sprang into action. Before the asshole could start the activation sequence, the dog grabbed his arm in his jaws and bit down hard. His scream echoed around the cabin, as Cam extracted the detonator from his bloody, clenched fingers.

It was over. They'd done it. None of the passengers would die. That's when the shock hit her, and she dropped onto the bunk, still clenching the bag with the VX.

"That was one hell of an entrance," Ryan said.

"It would have taken us longer if Chrissy hadn't sent us your exact location," Jake answered as he cuffed the only terrorist still standing.

"She did?"

"Yeah, she put a tracker on you. From the looks of you, she probably saved your sorry ass."

Ryan met her eyes. They looked like large brown buttons in her pale face. She still held the black bag in a death grip, but she was in one piece. Not a drop of her own blood spilled.

"That's right, Pooky. I saved your sorry ass," she echoed Jake and grinned.

"Wait, did she just call you Pooky?" Murph chortled.

"Fuck. You can forget you heard that."

"No way in hell, bro. It's too good."

Chrissy grinned again. Yeah, his hellion saved his ass. For the first time in his life, he'd been the one that needed to be rescued, and she'd been the one to do it.

"Let me take a look at you, bro," Rafe said before Ryan could say anything else.

"I'm fine. It looks worse than it is."

"Right." Rafe pushed him gently into a chair.

Ryan didn't need Rafe to examine him. He was the medic. They'd gotten in a couple of good punches and he had at least one fractured rib. The rest was just soft tissue. It would bruise, he'd be sore and look like shit, but in a few days he'd be fine. The rib would take about six weeks to be cleared for duty. He was lucky.

"You need to check, Chrissy. One of them, punched her in the stomach and he didn't hold back."

"Who is this guy?" Jake asked as he cuffed Reza.

"He's the ship's security officer," Chrissy answered. "Can you believe that shit. He's in charge too, at least for this group, but I'd bet he's the reason they could come and go so easily."

"Did you say Reza?"

"Yeah, why?

"If I'm right, the CIA has been trying to track him down for at least two years."

"They can have him, but I think I broke his jaw, so he probably won't be speaking anytime soon."

"You did?" Murph asked as the SEALs turned her way.

"She did," Ryan answered. "He never knew what hit him. After watching her in action, I'm really tempted to learn Krav Maga. She took him out in three moves."

"Fuck, really?"

"No shit?" Cam said.

"I did tell you I could take care of myself."

"Yes, you did," Jake answered for all of them.

The FBI really didn't know what an amazing woman they had. Once their report was submitted, Ryan had a feeling the CIA would try to recruit her.

At some point, Rafe had taken the black bag

from Chrissy. When they'd verified that it was the VX, he took pictures and sent them to JSOC then zipped it into a lead-lined bag with the disabled detonator. Mission complete.

"We need to get these tangos up to deck ten so we can hand them over to the Coasties," Jake said.

"So, Ryan, do you want to stay on the ship and finish your relaxing cruise?" Murph asked as he hefted one of the HVTs over his shoulder.

"No thanks. I'm really not that fond of cruising. How about you, Chrissy?"

"Nope, the faster I get off this ship, the better." Cam laughed as he helped her up.

"Halo, you are my hero. You were amazing and I love you," she said as she bent over to pet him and kissed him on the head, and Ryan was surprised that he was actually jealous of the dog.

"Want to come help me get the stuff from the cabin? I'll get yours too, Ryan."

The dog woofed as if he knew what she'd asked.

"Thanks," he said with a smile. His face felt stiff from the dried blood and his smile probably looked more like a grimace. It didn't seem to bother her though. His hellion was something else.

"Good idea. Halo, go with Chrissy. Keep her safe," Cam told the dog before grabbing one of the terrorists and slinging him over his shoulder.

Ryan watched Chrissy walk down the passageway with Halo, then followed his teammates carrying the VX to the chopper. The sooner he got off the ship the happier he'd be.

EPILOGUE

The CIA met them when the chopper landed in Norfolk. The Black Eagle team was more than happy to turn over the HVTs to them for interrogation. Although, Chrissy had been correct, she'd broken Reza's jaw and he wouldn't be talking for a while. They also took the VX. Ryan hoped they'd destroy it, but figured it was more likely to go into storage somewhere.

Ryan wrapped his ribs once they got to Little Creek. He'd have to get x-rays to make sure, but it wasn't the first time he'd had fractured ribs, he knew the drill, and it could wait until they were done being debriefed.

He needed to talk to Chrissy, but between the CIA and the mission debrief there hadn't been time. She'd been amazing, like a block of ice when the shit hit the fan. He owed her a million apologies, along with a full explanation, for his behavior over the past year.

It was only two days after they'd left from the Port, and yet it seemed like his entire life had been upended. All of his hardcore beliefs were proven wrong and he wasn't sure how to deal with it. It was times like this that he wished his mom was still alive, she'd always known the right thing to say. Too bad he hadn't listened to her all those years when she pleaded with him to open his heart. Somehow he'd found the perfect woman for him, and he hadn't been looking. She'd left without saying goodbye or saying anything.

"Where did Chrissy go?" he asked after he got back from talking to Captain Knox.

"Her boss called her in. They need their own debrief. She said and I quote, 'I'll talk to you later, Pooky,'" Murph said and made kissing noises. One of these days he was going to fall hard, and they'd never let him live it down.

"You suck balls," Ryan said and grimaced when he turned too quickly.

"Ryan, get yourself to the hospital," Jake commanded.

"I would, except my truck is at the cruise terminal."

"No problem. Rafe you and Murph go get Ryan's truck and bring it to the hospital. I'll drive you over. Cam, you and Halo can hit the road."

"Thanks, Boss."

"Captain Knox said we all have a week off. Let's hope it sticks this time. I could sure use the downtime."

"Copy that."

Two hours later, Ryan got the results he'd expected. Two fractured ribs, possible concussion, and the rest of his injuries were soft tissue. He didn't even get any stitches this time around. Considering the mission, he wasn't about to complain about a little rib pain.

Rafe and Murph brought his truck to the ER and stayed with him for a bit. He told Rafe to go home to Meghan, and Murph left shortly after Ryan turned him down for a drink. This was one time he didn't want to sit in the Ready Room and drink beer.

Driving home by way of Chrissy's, he was surprised to see that her place was still dark, and her Jeep wasn't there. Maybe she was with Rafe and Meghan, unless she was still at the FBI for her debrief.

Ryan parked in the lot in front of his apartment, grabbed his bag and locked the truck. His ass dragged as he gingerly stepped toward his front door. This time when he opened the door he didn't feel peace, instead it was dark, quiet, and lonely. He and Chrissy barely spent a day together in the same suite, yet he missed everything about her. Her scent. Her giggles. Her bad jokes. Hell, he even missed being called Pooky, not that he'd admit it out loud.

Still covered with dried blood, he needed a shower, a beer, and bed. The rest he'd deal with tomorrow. After flipping on the bathroom light and catching a glimpse of himself, he laughed, which immediately turned into a groan as his ribs reminded him they were fractured. No wonder he'd been getting weird looks everywhere he went, he looked like an extra from a horror movie.

The shower went a long way to soothing his aches. The two beers took it further, but he couldn't stop thinking about Chrissy. She'd left

Little Creek and that was that. Had he read her wrong? They'd agreed to the truce for the duration of the mission. Maybe it's how she dealt with the truce. But that kiss... Her reactions couldn't have been fake, he refused to believe that. He needed answers. Fuck. He needed to know she was okay.

Deciding to send her a text, he took out his phone just as it rang.

"Chrissy? Are you okay?"

"Of course. Why wouldn't I be?"

Good question, she had seemed fine, but she'd also almost killed a man. "You dealt with a lot of shit today and got punched in the stomach."

"Yeah, that asshole took me by surprise. I'm fine, no worries. Are you hungry?"

His stomach growled in response. The last thing he'd eaten were the muffins on the ship about fourteen hours earlier. "I didn't realize it until you asked, but I could definitely eat." Her muffled laughter triggered his smile. He'd never noticed that she laughed so much. Had his attitude brought out the obstinate hellion in her?

"Great. Open the door then."

"What?"

"I'm outside holding two pizzas. Unless, you..."

He didn't give her a chance to finish and let her in as quickly as he could cross the apartment to open the door. His focus was on one thing, seeing for himself she was fine. The pizza was a close second though.

Opening the door, he realized what he was wearing or not wearing—clothing. He'd re-wrapped his ribs and put on a pair of boxers after his shower. More of him was visible than ever before. Chrissy's cheeks flushed a lovely shade of rose and her eyes opened wide as her gaze traveled the length of him. Trouble was, the length grew the longer she stared.

"You really didn't have to dress up just for me," she commented and handed him the pizza boxes.

"I didn't think I'd be having company. Let me go put some clothes on."

"Don't do it on my account. I'm enjoying the eye candy."

"Damn, woman. Keep that up and you're going to make me blush. Cam is the eye candy of our team."

"Maybe for Miranda, but he's too young for me."

He didn't know what to say to that, so he kept his mouth shut and put the pizza on the coffee table, then went to get a couple of plates. "Do you want a beer or some wine?"

"Whatever you're having is fine."

"I'm having beer. I have wine, it's no problem."

"Okay, I'll take the wine."

Smiling since he'd already poured her a glass by the time she answered, he handed her the wine and a plate. "I'm guessing that you didn't bring two pizzas for me to eat by myself."

"No, I planned on inviting myself to dinner. We have some unfinished business."

Two beers down and a pain pill in the hospital later, his mind wasn't the sharpest. What business? Sex? Words? He didn't know. Rather than stick his foot in his mouth, he opened one of the boxes and inhaled. She'd brought his favorite meat lover's pizza.

"You're more than welcome and thank you for bringing this box of heaven. It was wise to bring two since I might be able to eat this pie on my own."

"I didn't think you'd eaten since the muffins. I'm glad I followed my instincts," she said as she grabbed a slice and laid it on her plate.

"Do you ever not follow it?" he asked between bites.

"Not really. Maybe in the beginning."

Devouring his first slice, he reached for a second before she'd even taken more than two bites. He might not be able to work puzzles like Chrissy, but he was damn good at reading people. There was something she wanted to say.

Putting down his plate, he took a swallow of beer and turned to her. "Okay, let's have it. I can feel your thoughts floating in the air like little stinging bugs."

"Really?"

'Yup. What's wrong?"

"I feel like we had a thing on the ship and I kind of don't want it to end. But I can't tell if it was real for you or just part of the mission." Her eyes focused on his face as she spoke, but by the time she'd finished, her gaze dropped to her plate.

Forgetting his ribs, he reached for her and moaned.

"Are you okay?"

"I'm fine, just some fractured ribs. Nothing I haven't dealt with before."

"Shit. I'm sorry."

"You have nothing to be sorry for, Chrissy. I have been sitting here wracking my brain wondering if you felt the same as I did. Then you show up here like an angel bearing pizza, and all I want to do is pull you into my arms and kiss you until you can't breathe.

"Thank God."

"Exactly how I feel, but I owe you an explanation. I've been a complete dick."

"You don't owe me anything. I haven't been all sweetness and light either. It was easier to be bitchy than admit the attraction."

"Yes, but you were afraid of how I'd react to you. For me, it was more important I didn't react to anyone." He had her full attention and it was almost impossible to resist the pull of her eyes. But he needed to explain.

"I'm not going anywhere," Chrissy replied as she picked up her plate and took a bite of the pizza.

"It's a long sad story, but I'll give you the short version. My brother married his high school sweetheart, Darlene, as soon as he graduated from college. I was a surprise baby and he was twelve years older than me. After nine-eleven he joined the marines and was deployed to Afghanistan."

From the look on her face, she had an idea of what was coming. But no matter how good she was at puzzles, he doubted she'd be expecting this ending.

"I know you've already figured out what happens next. Darlene was about eight months pregnant when they came to the door of my parents' house since she was staying with us. The news sent her into early labor, and she lost the baby."

"Oh no," Chrissy exclaimed, and her eyes filled with tears.

"My parents buried the baby two days after Patrick's funeral. It was too much for Darlene. My mother tried to help her, but one morning they found her dead, with an empty bottle of sleeping pills the doctor had prescribed, and a note."

Chrissy reached for him, but he held up his hand to stop her.

"Let me finish first."

She nodded.

"After losing all three of them, the joy drained out of my mother. She tried. She really did, but it was such a huge loss. I was thirteen when all of that happened, and I made a vow that I would never cause that kind of despair to anyone I loved. Women deserved to have a loving husband to protect them. Not one who went off to war and never come back.

Over the years my mother's happiness slowly came back, and she tried to convince me that I was wrong about love. That it was always worth the sacrifice, no matter how long it lasted. But I couldn't get the look of Darlene's face out of my head, the pure devastation. It gutted me every time I thought about her. So, I closed myself off, or did, until I met you. Somehow you managed to find the cracks in my armor."

"Oh my God, I'm so sorry. I can't even imagine how that must have felt. And yet you went on to become a Navy SEAL."

"I needed to avenge my brother's death. At some point it became more than that."

She nodded in understanding. "Thank you for telling me. But you have nothing to apologize for. Neither of us were on our best behavior. All of our friends saw what we couldn't."

"That's the truth. Rafe has been driving me crazy since I admitted you were hot."

Pink tinged her cheeks at his words. "You think I'm hot?"

"Did you not see my hard-on when you got here?"

"Yeah, I did, but I wanted to hear it again."

Ryan laughed, not as he wanted, but as much as his ribs allowed. Then in his best Fat Bastard impersonation from the Austin Power's movies, he said, "You're dead sexy."

"You keep that up, Pooky, and I might just fall in love with you."

"Might?"

"Yeah. Haven't you figured me out yet? You're definitely going to have to say it first."

She'd proved to him that love was possible. She'd saved him from the HVTs and from himself, knocking down his walls and letting the sunlight in. No doubt they would have their arguments, but it would be worth it. He only wished his mom could have met her.

"Come here." At first she hesitated, then moved closer to him on the couch and kneeled so she was at eye level. "I'm going to kiss you now, any objections?"

Instead of answering him, she placed her hands on either side of his bruised face and pulled him toward her. Their kiss was gentle at first, but as the passion sizzled between them he couldn't stop from pulling her onto his lap.

When her lips separated from his, the loss hit him in the gut. They'd come close to losing each other on that cruise ship and he hadn't told her how he felt. That couldn't happen again.

Gently he kissed her forehead and then tipped her face up so he could look her in the eyes. "Chrissy Stillwell, puzzle solver extraordinaire, my hellion, I love you and will until the day I die."

Her smile filled his apartment with light and relief flooded his body. "I love you too, Pooky."

Six weeks later...

It was pizza and game night at Rafe and Meghan's, Murph and Jake arrived first, as usual Cam, Halo and Miranda were last. Ryan and Chrissy were away. They'd left as soon as Ryan was told he wouldn't be evaluated for active duty for at least six weeks.

No one but Jake knew where they were, but it was okay. That the two most stubborn people they knew had finally come to their senses had been the best news ever. Well, that and thwarting a VX gas attack that could have wiped out a major city.

There hadn't been a mission since then, and the team was getting restless. Daily PT every morning, running practice missions the rest of the day got old. Not that they'd tell that to their women.

Jake had just grabbed another slice when his phone vibrated. At ten p.m. on a Friday night, it probably wasn't a social call. Seeing who it was, he got up and went into the other room.

"Hey Tex, what's up? Working late on a Friday."

"Eh, you know me."

"Yes, I do. Is there a problem?"

"Not sure I'd call it that. Maybe time for a solution?" Tex said.

"You fucking found Azfaar?"

"Yeah. He's in Afghanistan again, holed up with some ISIS and Al Qaeda fighters."

"Holy hell, I'm surprised he went back there. The Taliban was not happy with him."

"Yeah, well, he took out his old war chief and is now running the area."

"Fuck. Can you send what you've got. I'll contact Knox and see if we can get cleared to go get the son of a bitch."

"Will do."

"And Tex, thanks, bro. We wouldn't have been able to find him without you."

After disconnecting the call, Jake took a deep breath. Finally they would be able to finish it. As long as Azfaar was out in the wild their team wasn't safe. He'd tried to take them out before. It was only a matter of time until he tried again.

Deciding to hold off telling the team until they were cleared for the mission, he grabbed another round of beers from the fridge and headed back into the living room.

Rafe looked up as he came back in. "Everything okay?"

"Yup, everything is just fine."

The End

ABOUT THE AUTHOR

Lynne St. James has been writing for as long as she can remember. She has series in several different genres including romantic suspense, new adult and paranormal. She lives in the mostly sunny state of Florida with her husband, an eighty-five-pound, fluffy, Dalmatian-mutt horse-dog, a small Yorkie-poo, and an orange tabby named Pumpkin who thinks he rules them all.

When Lynne's not writing happily-ever-afters, which is hardly ever, she's drinking coffee and either reading or crocheting.

Where to find Lynne:

Email: lynne@lynnestjames.com

Amazon: https://amzn.to/2sgdUTe

BookBub: https://www.bookbub.com/authors/lynne-st-james

Facebook: https://www.facebook.com/authorLynneStJames

Website: http://lynnestjames.com

Instagram: https://www.instagram.com/lynnestjames/

Pinterest: https://www.pinterest.com/lynnestjames5

VIP Newsletter sign-up: http://eepurl.com/bT99Fj

BOOKS BY LYNNE ST. JAMES

Black Eagle Team

SEAL's Spitfire: Special Forces: Operation Alpha, Book 1

SEAL's Sunshine: Special Forces: Operation Alpha, Book 2

SEAL's Hellion: Special Forces: Operation Alpha, Book 3

Red Falcon Team

SEAL's Temptation, Book 1 (coming soon)

Beyond Valor

A Soldier's Gift, Book 1

A Soldier's Forever, Book 2

A Soldier's Triumph, Book 3

A Soldier's Protection, Book 4

A Soldier's Pledge, Book 5

A Soldier's Destiny, Book 6

A Soldier's Homecoming, Book 7 (coming soon)

A Soldier's Redemption, Book 8 (coming Soon)

Raining Chaos

Taming Chaos

Seducing Wrath

Music under the Mistletoe – A Raining Chaos Christmas (Novella)

Tempting Flame

Anamchara

Embracing Her Desires

Embracing Her Surrender

Embracing Her Love

The Vampires of Eternity

Twice Bitten Not Shy

Twice Bitten to Paradise

Twice Bitten and Bewitched

Want to be one of the first to learn about Lynne St. James's new releases? Sign up for her newsletter filled with exclusive VIP news and contests! http://eepurl.com/bT99Fj

There are many more books in this fan fiction world than listed here, for an up-to-date list go to www.AcesPress.com

You can also visit our Amazon page at: http://www.amazon.com/author/operationalpha

Special Forces: Operation Alpha World

Christie Adams: Charity's Heart
Denise Agnew: Dangerous to Hold
Shauna Allen: Awakening Aubrey
Brynne Asher: Blackburn
Linzi Baxter: Unlocking Dreams
Jennifer Becker: Hiding Catherine
Alice Bello: Shadowing Milly
Heather Blair: Rescue Me
Anna Blakely: Rescuing Gracelynn
Amy Briggs: Saving Sarah
Julia Bright: Saving Lorelei
Victoria Bright: Surviving Savage
Cara Carnes: Protecting Mari
Kendra Mei Chailyn: Beast
Melissa Kay Clarke: Rescuing Annabeth
Samantha A. Cole: Handling Haven
Sue Coletta: Hacked

Melissa Combs: Gallant
Anne Conley: Redemption for Misty
KaLyn Cooper: Rescuing Melina
Liz Crowe: Marking Mariah
Sarah Curtis: Securing the Odds
Jordan Dane: Redemption for Avery
Tarina Deaton: Found in the Lost
KL Donn: Unraveling Love
Riley Edwards: Protecting Olivia
PJ Fiala: Defending Sophie
Nicole Flockton: Protecting Maria
Michele Gwynn: Rescuing Emma
Casey Hagen: Shielding Nebraska
EM Hayes: Gambling for Ashleigh
Desiree Holt: Protecting Maddie
Kathy Ivan: Saving Sarah
Jesse Jacobson: Protecting Honor
Silver James: Rescue Moon
Becca Jameson: Saving Sofia
Kate Kinsley: Protecting Ava
Heather Long: Securing Arizona
Gennita Low: No Protection
Kirsten Lynn: Joining Forces for Jesse
Margaret Madigan: Bang for the Buck
Kimberly McGath: The Predecessor
Rachel McNeely: The SEAL's Surprise Baby

KD Michaels: Saving Laura
Wren Michaels: The Fox & The Hound
Kat Mizera: Protecting Bobbi
Mary B Moore: Force Protection
LeTeisha Newton: Protecting Butterfly
Angela Nicole: Protecting the Donna
MJ Nightingale: Protecting Beauty
Sarah O'Rourke: Saving Liberty
Victoria Paige: Reclaiming Izabel
Anne L. Parks: Mason
Debra Parmley: Protecting Pippa
Lainey Reese: Protecting New York
TL Reeve and Michele Ryan: Extracting Mateo
Elena M. Reyes: Keeping Ava
Angela Rush: Charlotte
Rose Smith: Saving Satin
Jenika Snow: Protecting Lily
Lynn St. James: SEAL's Spitfire
Dee Stewart: Conner
Harley Stone: Rescuing Mercy
Jen Talty: Burning Desire
Megan Vernon: Protecting Us

Police and Fire: Operation Alpha World

Freya Barker: Burning for Autumn
KaLyn Cooper: Justice for Gwen

Aspen Drake: Sheltering Emma

Deanndra Hall: Shelter for Sharla

Barb Han: Kace

CM Steele: Guarding Hope

Reina Torres: Justice for Sloane

Stacey Wilk: Stage Fright

As you know, this book included at least one character from Susan Stoker's books. To check out more, see below.

SEAL of Protection: Legacy Series

Securing Caite
Securing Brenae (novella)
Securing Sidney
Securing Piper
Securing Zoey (Jan 2020)
Securing Avery (May 2020)
Securing Kalee (Sept 2020)

Delta Team Two Series

Shielding Gillian (Apr 2020)
Shielding Kinley (Aug 2020)
Shielding Aspen (Oct 2020)
Shielding Riley (TBA)
Shielding Devyn (TBA)
Shielding Ember (TBA)
Shielding Sierra (TBA)

Delta Force Heroes Series

Rescuing Rayne (FREE!)

Rescuing Aimee (novella)
Rescuing Emily
Rescuing Harley
Marrying Emily (novella)
Rescuing Kassie
Rescuing Bryn
Rescuing Casey
Rescuing Sadie (novella)
Rescuing Wendy
Rescuing Mary
Rescuing Macie (Novella)

Badge of Honor: Texas Heroes Series

Justice for Mackenzie (FREE!)
Justice for Mickie
Justice for Corrie
Justice for Laine (novella)
Shelter for Elizabeth
Justice for Boone
Shelter for Adeline
Shelter for Sophie
Justice for Erin
Justice for Milena
Shelter for Blythe
Justice for Hope

Shelter for Quinn
Shelter for Koren
Shelter for Penelope

SEAL of Protection Series

Protecting Caroline (FREE!)
Protecting Alabama
Protecting Fiona
Marrying Caroline (novella)
Protecting Summer
Protecting Cheyenne
Protecting Jessyka
Protecting Julie (novella)
Protecting Melody
Protecting the Future
Protecting Kiera (novella)
Protecting Alabama's Kids (novella)
Protecting Dakota

New York Times, *USA Today* and *Wall Street Journal* Bestselling Author Susan Stoker has a heart as big as the state of Tennessee where she lives, but this all American girl has also spent the last fourteen years living in Missouri, California, Colorado, Indiana, and Texas. She's married to a retired Army man who now gets to follow *her* around the country.

www.stokeraces.com
www.AcesPress.com
susan@stokeraces.com

Made in the USA
Middletown, DE
05 November 2019

78048054R00124